Soul Bound II:
The Wounded
The Soul Bound Trilogy

By Jas T. Ward

Ink-N-Flow Publishing — Texas

<u>Also By Jas T. Ward</u>

Bits and Pieces: Tales and Sonnets

<u>The Shadow-Keepers Series</u>

CANDYMAN: Before the Madness

MADNESS

BOUNCE

LUST

COWBOY

MURDER

ENVY – *Coming January 2020*

<u>Romance – The Ward Way</u>

Love's Bitter Harvest

A Little Pill Called Love

<u>Soul Bound Trilogy</u>

Soul Bound I: The Warrior

Soul Bound II: The Wounded

Soul Bound III: The Wanted – *Coming April 2020*

Dedication:

To those lost souls still walking among us.
You will be seen. Scream until you are.

To All of Those Souls Bound to Souls That Are Gone.
Fight. And know you are not alone.

- Jas

PROLOGUE

"Amanda! For fuck's sake, you have to stop this!" He tried to pull her hand away from her thigh, but it once again, happened so quick, the damage was done. He only wanted to hold her hand in hopes to connect with her and released her arm to do so—a mistake that would cost him. Yelling for help, he pinned his wife's arms to the armrests to stop her from hurting herself. Her doing so increased in frequency to more than a dozen times over the last week alone. The nurses arrived to assist in less than a minute. Amanda fought like a person possessed, despite the so-called "best in the mental health field" telling him that was bullshit.

Standing back as they used the leather and wool arm restraints, he couldn't take his eyes away from the bloody markings on his wife's white thigh. They were deep gouges in her flesh with crimson running down to stain the folded sheet she sat upon in the wheelchair. Letting out a snarl of frustration, he could already tell she was sickly driven to once again carve the same word in her skin—CAMDEN. He could make out the bloody C she had achieved. Turning away as Amanda thrashed and screamed, he knew they would sedate her again. However, if allowed to finish her obsessed task, she would have just fallen back into whatever void her mind fell into without chemical assistance. Nothingness was all she would experience without the mercy of unconsciousness. She had lost so much weight from neither eating nor drinking—they told him that they would have to put in a feeding tube if she didn't come out of her unresponsive state.

A state that only changed when she tried to carve that fucking word.

"Mr. Bishop?"

He was in the process of lighting a cigarette with a trembling hand when one of the doctors joined him outside of the mental hospital. Giving the man an angry scowl, he braced himself for whatever tidbit of bullshit was about to be verbally tossed at him next. He had a small moment of victory when he succeeded in lighting the cigarette in the brisk Cleveland wind. It was getting colder as it swept over Lake Erie; white capping the waves on the huge expanse of water. Blowing out a slow exhale of breath and smoke, he pivoted to address the doctor. "What? Are you going to tell me you want to do another useless scan of her brain? Take another tube of blood that won't tell you a damn thing? Go for it. It's not like it will reveal anything, but why not piss in the wind again for the advancement of research's sake?"

The doctor cleared his throat, turning his head to avoid the smoke. "Actually, we may have found the source of the word your wife has been mutilating on her body. But it's not exactly a word."

Steven turned to give the doctor his full attention now. Finally, something that could help them to solve the mystery his wife had become since the car wreck that landed them both in the icy lake two months ago. It had been strange—Amanda suffered severe hypothermia and upon being resuscitated, she fell into a deep coma. Or so they thought until the first of these "episodes." This new twist with the bloody word had started a month or so ago. Flicking the cigarette away, he narrowed his eyes. "Okay, so it's not a word. What is it?"

The doctor stiffened as if he braced for a fight and cleared his throat again in nervousness. "It's a name."

CHAPTER ONE

"We shouldn't have done it, Sky."

Kitt Thomas sat on the bottom stair step, a beer bottle dangling from her fingers as a beautiful sunset colored the sky in pastels of blue and pink. Taking a long draw on the Bud, she glanced over at her best friend. "It was all such a mistake. How are we ever going to get past it and be able to live with ourselves? What we did to Jace?"

Skylar Williams blew out a slow breath and shrugged. "We did what we thought needed to be done, Kitt. It was the only choice we had. How could we know it would go so horribly wrong?" She reached out to touch Kitt's arm. "Why don't you go inside, get some rest if you can. You're looking exhausted."

Kitt swiveled her head to regard the lovely brunette—a best friend to her and Jace Camden. But a title they all held now whether anyone knew or not was "accessory to murder."

Kitt had no idea what steps Skylar had carried out to cover it all up. Just like having no idea what additional moves it took for Alexis Martinez or Franklin Wormwood to assist in that cover up of what they all had done. All Kitt knew to be fact in that moment was that the beer was cold, and it was true to her in its simplistic existence in her life. When it stopped numbing her, there was a bottle of Maker's Mark ready to offer its clarity.

But Skylar was right. She was exhausted. Kitt just could not get it out of her head—that night. It played over and over. What they had all done...

When they had killed the man she loved.

Jace Camden.

"She's still pissed, huh?"

Skylar turned back as Kitt actually went upstairs as asked as Jace Camden and Zane Miller arrived. Snorting, she scooted over to let both men join her on the stairs that led to Jace's beach house. "Yes. Your girlfriend is extremely stubborn." She angled her head to regard him and smiled. "So, dead guy who is no longer dead, what did the doctor say?" She was slightly joking, but the mileage on giving Jace shit about having to die and then coming back wasn't even close to expiring. The humor assisted them all in hiding the worry they still carried for Jace. It had not helped that since the night they had cheated his permanent death, Jace had been getting headaches and nosebleeds. He didn't seem very concerned, though. He told Skylar he'd happily exchange those two symptoms for no longer getting his ass kicked in his sleep and not being a chew toy for demons.

"The doctor said his heart is as weird as he is," Zane summarized simply.

Both she and Jace glanced back at the man. Jace let out a chuckle as he reached over to take Sky's beer and took a big swig. "I believe that's Zane's evaluation. They did not say that unless he is now a mind-reader." Zane began to speak but Jace cut him off. "That's not at all what they said. Alex and the doc believe it's just blood pressure related. They heard unusual beats and found some odd scarring on my heart wall that seems recent." He raised a brow followed by a sardonic smile as he handed the bottle back, "but no heart attack. Nothing to be concerned about. Considering my recent…ah…events, it most likely will clear up on its own."

Jace let out a chuckle as he let his gaze shift upward to the house, where he could hear footsteps on the floor above. "You should have seen how good Alex is getting at hiding the truth within believable half-truths without telling a single lie. She told her colleague I had an accidental overdose, coded, and she was personally monitoring me along with Franklin. You can imagine my joy at anyone thinking that. But what's wrong? Nothing that they could find. The usual round-about bullshit medical way of saying they have no idea."

Skylar listened to her friend and darted a look at Zane, who simply gave a shrug—as usual, no help whatsoever on anything that mattered. Picking at the label of her bottle, she reached out to take Jace's hand and squeezed it in hers. "Are you sure we shouldn't be more worried? I know you've told me a dozen times it's over, but then you have one of those episodes where your big ole nose starts leaking valuable red liquid that your body might need and I doubt your reassurances." She smirked. "Not to mention, the last time you did it all over my new couch. Blood stains, dead guy. Even if it is leather upholstery."

Jace squeezed her hand back, leaned over, and kissed her cheek. "I replaced the couch. Goodwill didn't seem to care that it looked like a prop straight out of a horror film." He stood and turned to go inside. "Wish me luck. I'm going in." Skylar tracked him, her sharp mind trying to detect a misstep, a weakness. Anything to cause her to worry that Jace was going to fall over dead.

Again.

Zane moved to sit next to her and she smacked him as he tried to make the same move as Jace had in reaching for her beer. He yelped and even pouted. "You are so mean. I did help lift that couch, you know." He bent an arm to flex his muscles and wiggled a brow at her. "The gun show is always open for you, Sky."

That got him yet another smack.

CHAPTER TWO

Jace entered the house and followed the music that played down the small hall. Pushing open the door, he leaned into the opening to watch Kitt completely ignore the laundry she had used as a ruse to cover her nervous fidgeting. "Hey."

His beautiful girlfriend looked up, rewarded him with a smile, and bounded off the bed to run at him. Kitt threw her arms and a leg around his to squeeze him tight. "What did the doctor say?"

Jace chuckled as he closed the door before shuffling them both over to the bed to drop her and then himself on top of the mound of clothes. He then returned her smile as he kissed her. "Just residual effects from what we pulled off. They didn't find anything and said to just take it easy for a bit. My blood pressure trying to be a bitch, most likely." He kissed her again before he rested on his forearms to look down at her. Frowning, he brought his fingers up to brush along her cheek. His Kitt was always tan and sun-kissed, but the shadows under her eyes gave him concern. "Did you get any rest?"

Kitt dismissed his question as she slid out from under him, rolled Jace to his back, and laid on top of him. Her fingers touched him in return by skirting along the scar on his chin that showed slightly through the scruff of his trimmed whiskers. Kitt knew how Jace had received it. In fact, she knew every single story that accompanied every single scar now. He was more than okay with that. God, how he loved his quirky, wacky beach girl.

"They said no worries? I mean, they checked everything, right? Did you tell them about the nosebleeds? The headaches?" She gave him a skeptical and scrutinizing look as her eyes narrowed. "Did you tell them how you sleep really, really deep? You never used to do that. Sure you had..."

Rather than answer relentless questions, Jace pulled her down and kissed her again. This time, he desired to give her tongue more to do than ramble on nervously about his health. Just like the marks on his body, Kitt knew he detested discussing doctors. Their presumed analysis and attempts to understand what made Jace—only to figure out not a single damn thing was his second least favorite topic. Being different took first position in sour topics. A mystery Jace dared to believe was no longer a factor.

He slept like a normal man. He had not seen, heard, or even glimpsed anything that didn't belong in the realm of reality for the first time since he was a kid. Sure, he knew that might not always be the case. After all, if what they had witnessed a few months ago, it had to. Bound too. All the soul warrior bullshit. Jace still had a very hard time believing any of it no matter how much effort Franklin, his friend and modern druid, put into the research. But for now... things were good. He had friends. He had gotten his license to drive back and most of all, he was completely, totally, without a single regret, in love with the woman who he now made out with like a teenager on their bed and a pile of clothes. His home, now Kitt's and Jace's, happiness was whole and complete.

He was in the process of shucking Kitt's t-shirt off when the sound of car doors sounded just outside the lower level of his beach house. "Jace," she whispered breathlessly against his lips, apparently also hearing the interruption. Whoever had arrived would wait. Kitt's salt kissed skin should never have to be put on hold. It and the taste of it under his tongue, a siren's call to Jace—a lonely sailor seeking the haven it promised.

Jace let out a deep rumbled moan within a kiss as his hand slid over her stomach. And a very different type of moan escaped him when a rapid knock struck against the closed bedroom door. The moment vaporizing through the shrill beckoning of Jace's very annoying psychiatrist, Alex. "Jace! Jace! I need to talk to you. It's important. Jace? Are you in there?"

He sighed and dropped his head to Kitt's shoulder. She shook with mirth and a soft laugh at the abrupt interruption of their "noon-er" sex.

"Are you sure he's in there? I don't hear him. Jace?"

Jace turned his head to listen as Franklin's voice told Alex to stop and reminded her what any couple would be doing in a bedroom with the door closed that could be quiet at first. Alex and the holistic healer then began debating whether sex was indeed taking place and well...

Kitt started laughing. It was time for the debate outside the door to end—like Jace's chance at getting laid.

"What?" Jace yelled in reply, a growl edging his voice, but then he let out a whimper when Kitt moved away, pulled on her tee, and opened the door. Lifting up to sit, Jace saw all four of his friends standing there. Zane stood in the rear of the group, craning to see around the others—most likely in hopes of catching a glimpse at Kitt's recently bare parts. Skylar was amused as always. Jace was pretty sure she had known what was going on. And then there were Alex and Franklin— they did not look happy at all. Sighing, Jace stood to move in front of the group in the doorway. "This better be important."

Alex nodded and glanced at Franklin for support before saying gravely, "It is. There's another one. Or the same one. But regardless, Jace, it's something you need to see." She held a printed photo out to him. He looked at it in puzzlement as he tried to understand what he saw. His head came up sharply in alarm when he realized what it showed.

Alex handed him more. "Whatever it is seems to be calling you out personally."

"Wait, slow down. None of this makes sense."

They gathered in the living room and surrounded the coffee table currently covered in boxes of pizza from The Big Store. A cold six-pack sat on the floor. Paper plates were heaped with slices waiting to be devoured, but primarily ignored and going cold. Jace held the photo printouts Alex had brought as he once again tried to digest and make reasonable sense of the images.

A woman. One he had never seen before, nor knew. She appeared in various states of restraint for her safety with one common detail in every shot—his name carved into her skin. Others showed the gory process halted after only a few letters. This particular detail really fucked with Jace's head, it appeared the damage was done from the *inside* out.

"I've never been to Cleveland. Or Ohio. Or in that fucking half of the country." Jace tossed the papers to the table and stood to pace. Jace stowed the information in his gray matter; what they knew and what they did not. "And she's in a coma? Except when *that* happens?

When she does it or..." He swallowed as a cold trickle of fear ran down his spine and mumbled, "something does that."

Alex fretted, biting her bottom lip, as she held a piece of pizza. It received intense scrutiny as if it was an alien food substance to her. Jace guessed either pizza was not his therapist's usual fare or doubts in play considering the topic of dinner conversation. Setting the slice down, she attempted to once again explain.

"It started a month ago." She shuffled through the photos and found a specific one and slid it to Jace. She pointed to the time stamp printed on the corner. "Look at the date, Jace. The time."

Blowing out a frustrated breath, Jace did as instructed and his stomach felt as if it dropped. His lungs decided they wanted nothing to do with any of this and locked up. Jace would actually have preferred passing out to this. He dropped down back in a chair. "Fuck... no fucking way."

He was a southern guy through-and-through. Which is why he had lived there his entire life. However, part of the reason was he really hated flying. The thought of being stuck inside of a metal tube with strangers felt like a convenient mass burial in a community coffin to Jace. Therefore, the fact that freaky ass shit of the nature he had hoped he would not have to think about occurred so far away only added to the nightmare quality of the facts. Ironic that nightmares were an area of his expertise. "Ohio. How the hell is this happening there? And then..."

Kitt moved over to sit on the arm of the chair to take the photo from him. "What are you two talking about?" But her words faltered a moment later and Jace could hear her breath catch as his had. "It happened at that very minute. That day." She met his eyes, and he found confused fear swimming in those blue depths. "The exact minute you came back to life. When we freed Laura. How is that even possible?"

She darted her eyes up to the others. "No one outside this room knows about that."

"Road trip!"

All eyes slid to Zane at his loud outburst. He had jumped to his feet and was fist-pumping the air with glee. Jace slapped a hand to his forehead as Kitt let out a groan. His two therapists both simply blinked as Zane behaved like an excited kid at the prospect of traveling.

Skylar walked up and smacked Zane hard on the back of the head with her palm. "We're not going to Disney World you idiot. This is not a good thing."

Zane squeaked, unsure as to why everyone else wasn't as thrilled as he was. "Oh, I get it. Airplane ride. I mean, Ohio to Texas is really far. It's like driving from almost Mexico to almost Canada, right? So, vroom! Dead Man Crew is hitting the skies!" He became giddier as he bounced on his sandaled feet. "We should get matching tees so we don't get lost in the airport." He pulled out his phone as he lowered to sit cross-legged on the floor. "We'll do rush shipping."

His hand went up and out to wiggle his fingers towards Jace. "Dude, give me your credit card."

CHAPTER THREE

"Dude, are you really afraid of flying? Seriously?"

Jace's head was down, focused on reading the patient's file notes Alex obtained from the woman's psychiatrist in Ohio. Zane had twisted around in the airplane seat in front of Jace to inquire into what should have been a closed subject. "Yes, Zane. I am. And you are not helping." He parked a pointed finger on the file and leveled a warning glare at his friend. "I'm trying to concentrate on anything *other* than the fact we might die a fiery death from 30,000 feet in the sky."

Jace had learned the woman's name was Amanda Bishop, and she was only twenty-eight years old. Married for five years to a man by the name of Steven. They had no children and Mrs. Bishop had zero history of mental illness and was employed as a kindergarten teacher. Mr. Bishop, the CEO of a small program management firm specializing in outsourcing resources via proposals to other companies, including government agencies. Each award and client proudly touted on the Bishop Agency's website. Judging by the public Facebook profiles of the couple, the Bishops were happy; smiling and living an ideal, suburban life. That had all tragically changed when she and her husband suddenly careened off the road in the small town of Sheffield Lake, Ohio, a few miles from Cleveland. Police reports stated no other vehicles were involved. Their car had plunged into Lake Eerie in the dead of night. Mr. Bishop avoided injury, but his wife had to be resuscitated and remained in a coma ever since. And according to the woman's social media, Amanda posted about being a homebody and they never traveled.

Jace found that reason a more positive spin for not having frequent flyer miles than his own of once having been on trial for murder, probation for assault, or locked up in a looney bin. His fear of flying didn't help either. The irony was not lost on Jace that none were true for him now. Mrs. Bishop had the type of life Jace once would have believed he'd never acquire. That is, until the past few months. The evolution of Jace's existence occurred partly in thanks to the beautiful woman who crashed into his nightmare of a life like a spotlight in his dark. Too bright and blinding for him to ignore even though he had stubbornly tried—even then, his Kitt chose to go into the darkness with him.

"Turn around in your seat Zane, or I'm going to sic Sky on you to make you behave," Jace commanded in a half-serious, half-joking manner as he pointed a finger at his friend to do what he was told like an impatient toddler, rather than a grown-ass man. Depending on Jace's mood, Zane added amusement to Jace's days. Other times, like today, he was more irritation than Jace wanted to deal with.

Zane went rigid in reaction to Jace's threat but relaxed to see that both Sky and Kitt waited in the line for the bathroom a plane aisle length away. Franklin and Alex sat three rows up and Jace knew both were reluctant to allow Jace access to the Bishops' file notes. He relied on the fact that Alex had informed the Bishop woman's doctor and husband in Ohio that he would be serving as consultant on her case. It was not like they could walk in there and tell them he was "the demon guy." To pull the deception off successfully, he needed to be educated on the same facts as Alex and Franklin. But the real reason Jace wanted the file was to attempt to discover at least one damn thing in common between him and the woman carving his name in her flesh. There was zero. Nothing.

Well, not exactly no commonalities; his name was Camden. And she wore scars of it. They had both died and been brought back. But so had hundreds if not millions on the planet. Why her?

Death came to the forefront in Jace's mind when Zane unfortunately did not do as asked and continued to speak. "I mean, you have..."

Jace let out an irritated sigh as Zane knelt beside his aisle seat and spoke in hushed tones. The man *seriously* could not take a damn hint. "You faced off against demons. Like…went toe-to-toe with them. Ugly, nasty demons. Well, when they aren't masquerading like hot women I'd bang, ugly. You might be the only one who has done that. And hundreds, heck, millions of people fly and there's not often a plane crash. What? Four, five a year? If that." Zane then leaned in closer to whisper, "One day we're going to talk about that demon sex, right? I have questions, dude."

Jace squeezed his eyes shut in frustration, rested an elbow on the arm rest, and pressed his hand over his face. "Zane, I swear…if you don't shut up, I'm cramming your ass in the overhead bin."

"Shut up, Zane. You make him puke about flying, I'm going to help him do that." Kitt rescued Jace as she stepped through to take her seat next to him. Skylar assisted in the rescue by corralling Zane back to his seat. Exhaling to ease his tension, Jace closed the file and slid it in the pocket on the back of Zane's seat. Resting his head sideways to rest on the top of Kitt's, he focused on her hand wrapping around his.

Lifting them, he regarded the amulet affixed to a leather cuff she wore on her wrist. Franklin had designed them so that all four of them could wear them and have the amulets in constant, close contact with their skin. Jace wasn't exactly sure how the protected items worked, but he did know demons hated whatever mumbo-jumbo infused the stone-looking pieces—and that was all that mattered. Keeping his friends safe was a comforting positive plus.

The negative in that protection was that the amulets had the opposite effect on Jace. If any of the amulets touched his skin, it would burn and sizzle as if he were a demonic threat. Just another personal mystery he would have to figure out along with the little documented warrior legend. The few facts the shaman-genius had uncovered regarding soul warriors were noted in an ancient book, which documented various druid and other pagan beliefs. Beyond that, the information they had to go on was frustrating, vague, and scant at best.

What Franklin stood solid on from his research involved the belief that only one such warrior could exist within the same generation. They supposedly could walk both within the realm of the living and the dead. Franklin believed that at the peak of a warrior's power, they might be able to reach the highest level of soul–that of the unborn or those destined for reincarnation. That is, if Franklin was correctly interpreting all the mystical mumbo-jumbo. Jace had yet to be convinced.

If those supernatural beliefs weren't baffling enough, Franklin was convinced the warriors were the only weapon that could save mankind from the demons that fed on human souls. Like the type that came too close to devouring his late wife, Laura's soul. Did those readings tell Franklin or Jace how to use them? How to fight the demons? No, of course not. That would have been too fucking easy. Jace never counted on easy. In fact, he questioned with a huge amount of cynicism anything that appeared to be. Life lessons—Camden 101. Jace should do a fucking Ted Talk on the subject of faith and reality.

"Find anything?"

Jace shook his head at Kitt's question as he brought her hand closer to kiss her wrist, careful not to touch the amulet. "Not a single thing. It makes no sense. And that worries me. There's already so much I don't know now, Kitt. And…" he turned to hunch down in the seat to her eye level, "I was enjoying the fact that maybe all this shit was over. Done. And I could finally have a life I never really thought I'd get a chance to have." His eyes went downward. "With you."

Kitt sighed and cupped a palm against his cheek. "I know, baby. That's why I thought this was a bad idea. But I also know you want to help." She pressed a gentle kiss against his lips and curled up as much as she could against him within the airline seat's tight confines. "Can I ask a favor? I know better than to ask you to promise." She added a smile that was both nervous and playful.

Jace snorted softly. Kitt knew his mood was sour and he found it cute she did her best not to send him further in that direction. "Sure. What flavor of a favor are we talking about, sweetheart?"

Kitt's gaze shifted to the file in front of them. "No playing with death this time." Her hand moved to rest on his chest and Jace knew she sought reassurance at the thumps of his heart beneath her fingers. "We help if we can, but no playing the hero. We still don't know everything about all this. And I really don't think I can handle watching you die again, okay?"

Jace tilted her chin up as his opposite hand covered hers. "Deal. I'm going as a consultant only." He laughed a bit. "You guys just refused to let me go without you. They pulled the whole friend card on me. Which I might appreciate and like." He smiled and moved his hand to show a finger and thumb a hair apart. "A little." He kicked the back of Zane's seat in front of him. "That goes for you too, buddy. Unless, of course, we die in a crash. Don't be worried. I've done dead before. It only hurts like hell for a minute."

That got him a smack from Kitt.

And a high-five over the seat from Zane.

CHAPTER FOUR

"One too many itty-bitty bottles of Jack, dude?"

Jace glared at Zane as his friend stood next to him at the sink in the men's room of the Cleveland, Ohio airport. "Shut up. Go away." Jace shoved him back as he cupped another handful of water to bring to his mouth to rinse it out; needed due to throwing up the moment they had touched down. Finding his travel bottle of mouthwash in his carry on, Jace swished it around and spit into the sink. Dropping it back in his bag, he turned to face Zane to find that even if the man made jokes, his features portrayed more concern. "You and the rest need to stop worrying about me. Shit."

Leaving the restroom, Jace was not surprised to find Skylar, Kitt, Franklin, and Alex giving him matching worried looks as well. "I got motion sickness. Nothing more. What next?" He smacked Franklin's hand away as the man reached out in an effort to take his wrist to check Jace's pulse. The annoying habit continued no matter how many smacks the move received. "Stop that. I am fine. Alex, where do we go?"

Alex chewed on her nail—a habit Jace liked to think he had nothing to do with in its development. They had become friends, even if Jace may have been her least compliant patient and she once took action to commit him to a facility. "I rented us a car. We need to pick it up. I already let Dr. Lewis know we're on our way."

Kitt wove her arm around Jace's waist and kissed his cheek as she punched him in the arm for being so cranky. Kitt's concern, Jace would tolerate. The others, no. "Then let's get this done. I want to go back home already."

"Doctor Martinez, it's a pleasure to meet you. I wish it was under more pleasant circumstances." Doctor Lewis reminded Jace of one of Texas' nuisance critters. An armadillo. They had pointy-faces, tiny legs, and had a death wish that made them cross hot highways and become road-kill. The man in front of him appeared to want to curl up into a ball whenever he sniffed or imagined some threat. At least armadillos had armored backs to protect them. Doctor Lewis, on the other hand, looked as if he wished he had protection. To make up for armor nature had not gifted him, Doctor Lewis kept a frayed yellow legal pad clutched against his chest instead. Jace found a great deal of internal amusement to wonder if the man would also curl into a ball if he yelled "boo".

Maybe he'd try that another day for entertainment.

Jace, Zane, and Kitt remained behind the others as introductions were made. His name was conveniently glossed over as he was simply introduced as "a consultant on the case." Zane, Skylar, and Kitt were labeled as "knowledge-based associates." Part of Jace wished the farce would end before it had a chance to begin. His anxiety rose the moment they stepped inside the deceptively posh mental health facility housing Amanda Bishop. No cold, antiseptic interior like those Jace had been committed to as a child and later as an adult. A privately-owned center, it reminded him of a fancy resort or recovery center. He even caught a glimpse of an indoor pool beyond the foyer that rivaled any at a five-star hotel. As Jace discretely processed the details of the place, he noted the staff dressed in soft pastel-hued scrubs. The clothing gave him the impression they were made by a fashion designer—created for visual appeal, rather than functional practicality.

Not at all the starched garments Jace associated with mental hospitals. His brain, at times not his friend, engaged to ensure he never forgot, as it dredged up memories of nurses in pure white nurse uniforms. How glaring the blood stood out when it spotted the cloth.

Kitt gave his hand a squeeze. The gesture forced his mind to recede from the jagged mental cliff it had inched to leap from. Jace swiveled his head downward to meet her eyes and received a nervous and understanding smile. Jace was unable to return it, but he did muster a nod in acknowledged gratitude. As Kitt tugged on their shared clasp, she said softly, "Stay with me, baby. Let's focus on this and then we can go home."

Glancing up, Jace found the others had moved yards away and with Kitt leading, he followed. They traveled down an equally fancy hallway and he noticed the doors had no windows. He could perceive no sound behind them.

Jace's steps faltered in the long hall of the series of doorways set equidistant apart and each door painted in different muted colors. Jace could not help but shiver at how much it reminded him of the nightmare realm. There, the doors were portals linked to the living. Held behind unmarked exteriors where nightmares manifested as diverse as the humans connected to the souls held within the interiors. There, demons fed.

Jace was sure the color-scheme here had been selected for its aesthetic appeal, but the similar effect to the realm churned his stomach and escalated his anxiety. A fine sheen of cold sweat broke out on his skin and his heart began to pound like a drum in his ear. Its volume louder than the permanent ringing due to damage to his eardrum from the gun going off so close to his head that tragic night years ago.

They reached one door and that's when the mental cliff loomed once again and his hand shot out to brace himself on the wall. The moment Jace touched its smooth surface he heard a hiss and the others gave no indication of hearing it. He jerked his palm away and ground his teeth as more sweat popped out on his forehead and scalp, dampening his hair. "There's a demon here."

Kitt looked over at him in alarm and stiffened in place. Zane moved in front of Skylar protectively as she glanced around anxiously. Franklin pulled out his amulet, which hung from a leather string on his neck and Alex fidgeted with one of the same on a bracelet. Forcing himself to regulate his breathing, Jace bent at the waist to rest his hands on his knees with his head down. "Kitt, you still have yours, right?"

She moved to rub his back and nodded. "I do. I promised I wouldn't take it off."

Jace still darted his eyes up to make sure. Not due to doubt, but needing reassurance even though mere hours had passed since the last time he checked on the plane. The only times Jace allowed—not without balking anyway— for Kitt to alter how she wore it was whenever they made love. Even then, it would still be worn, but encased in a leather pouch Franklin had designed. It allowed Jace and Kitt to be skin-to-skin during sex and when sleeping. The latter was invaluable to Jace—he only slept worth a damn with Kitt wrapped around him as tight as possible.

Doctor Lewis appeared puzzled at Jace's obviously bizarre behavior and regarded the group. "Excuse me, Doctor Martinez, is your consultant unwell?"

Skylar gave the man a nervous smile with a slight head shake. "He did not have a good flight, nor much sleep. Perhaps we should give him a few hours at the hotel to recover."

"No. I don't want to be here longer than we have to." Jace replied with a strained voice. He swallowed the bile and nausea as he straightened his posture and did his best to compose himself. He hadn't felt the bewildering, sickening sensation of being close to evil since returning to life after freeing Laura's soul. Jace had been a fool to think the darkness that caused this effect had forgotten his existence. He only hoped it was not an indicator that he had been set up to come here.

Doctor Lewis keyed a code into the security pad by the door and the door popped open. As a group, they moved into an observation area as the door clicked securely behind them. Jace and the others faced a huge window. He presumed it was constructed as one-way glass. Beyond it, could be seen a more traditional holding room. Complete with padded walls.

In the middle sat a young woman secured in a wheelchair by restraints at her wrists and ankles. A long string of drool ran from her languid lips, her body's slumped posture reminding Jace of a worn, well-used ragdoll. She faced the observation glass and her eyes were vacant. In fact, the only indicator that she still lived was a shallow, rapid pant. Its fast rise and fall fluttering reminded Jace of a frantic, trapped butterfly. One that drew Jace in closer—he wanted to set it free. Her pale skin was as white as her doctor's lab coat. But it was the contrasting dark red cuts on her arm that captured his horrified scrutiny.

"That's my name." In ragged letters, 'CAMDEN' was carved into her skin. It was horrifying to try to comprehend how it could have happened. "I don't know her. I've never met her. How is this?" Jace brought up shaking hands to comb his fingers through his hair. "Fuck me."

Doctor Lewis moved to stand next to him while Alex took a position on the opposite side. "Your name?" The man glanced over at Alex and Jace in shock. "You are *that* Camden? Dr. Martinez, this is *your* patient?"

Alex went to reply when suddenly the door behind them flew open and Jace was jerked back and slammed against a wall. Jace let out a snarl. Ready to fight by learned survival instinct when Doctor Lewis rushed over to get in the way. The man who attacked Jace was in his face. A furious glare on his features.

"You're Camden? Who the *hell* are you?!" Jace was pulled forward, only to be shoved to the wall a second time. "Why the fuck is my *wife* clawing your name into her *skin?!*"

The realization this was the woman's husband and kindred sympathy for the man overtook Jace's own aggression. It was a welcoming release from his crippling confusion. He let out a breath as he eased his hands from fists to understanding palms on the man's arms. "I have no idea. But I plan on finding out."

CHAPTER FIVE

"So, you think my wife is possessed?"

The laughter from Steven Bishop that followed came as no surprise to Jace. Years ago, Jace would have been the same way, so there would be no judging of the man from him. "Not possessed in a church, sprinkle some holy water kind of way, no. To be honest with you," Jace leaned against a wall in Doctor Lewis' office as Bishop paced the room, reminding Jace more of his former self. "I'm not sure what is going on with your wife. But have you gotten any answers? I'm going to bet not or else I wouldn't have been brought here."

Bishop stopped his back-and-forth pacing to narrow his gaze at Jace. "You're not a doctor. You're not even a professional. What kind of bullshit is this?" He directed his acidic attitude towards Doctor Lewis. "I pay a shitload of money to have my wife a patient here. To get the best care--and you call in a snake oil salesman?"

Franklin snorted from his place on the sofa with Skylar sitting on the arm. "If anyone is the snake oil salesman here, that's *my* role on the team," he stated as he pressed a hand on his chest with a jolly, nonplussed smile. "We all have our roles. I shall take that one as the team hippie."

Alex scolded Franklin with a reproachful look over her glasses before she pushed them up her nose and addressed Mr. Bishop. "I know how you feel. Believe me, it's an understatement for me to declare that both Mr. Camden and my associate, Doctor Wormwood had a very difficult time convincing me that not all things can be explained by diagnosis and textbooks. But Mr. Camden is accurate. If I did not believe he could help, I would not have him here to do so." She removed her glasses. Jace looked away with a smirk as she stepped closer to Bishop. He knew what was coming next.

"I want to help you. We all do. So let us do that, Mr. Bishop."

And there it was—that gentle, yet firm tone paired with the "help me help you" expression. Jace had recognized that particular manipulation tool in Alex's professional skillset in his initial appointment with her. Bishop appeared not to buy it any more than Jace had all those months ago.

"Help me? Really? You're a fucking shrink, right? Don't you need my wife to actually tell you something? To be able to speak to you?" Bishop threw his arm outward to the side towards the direction of his wife's room. "Did you see her? Does she look ready to lay back on a couch and tell you about traumas from her childhood? Blame her mother, who is dead, for your information, for how fucked up she is? No." Bishop backed away, pivoted, and headed for the door to leave. "Do whatever you want, but the moment I feel like my decisions are being disobeyed on how to care for my wife, it stops."

With that and the door slam which followed, Bishop made his demands and left.

Alex pulled her glasses down with a sigh and asked the obvious. "What does he mean 'decisions?' What are we dealing with, Dr. Lewis?"

Bishop's physician took a seat, his lips meshing together to form a thin, stressed line. "He wants her transferred into hospice care and all recovery methods ended. He believes she's gone and no restoration to a quality of life is possible."

Jace stared to the side as the doctor spoke and pushed off the wall to confront when he had stopped speaking. "Are you fucking kidding me? He's not even wanting to find out? To not fight for her?" He ground his teeth and snorted in disbelief. "So basically, he wants her to die."

Doctor Lewis shook his head and regarded Jace forlornly. "No, Mr. Camden. He believes she's already dead."

"Jace, you need to relax."

His head rested on Kitt's lap as her fingers gently brushed through his hair. They had returned to the hotel. The moment they entered the room, Skylar entered into "legal eagle" mode on her laptop as she focused like the winged predator to find her prey. Zane played some game on his phone and they all awaited Alex and Franklin's return from the hospital with any more information they could gleam from Dr. Lewis.

A pounding migraine had set up in Jace's skull on the way back and the usual bloody nose that followed the episode tickled his sinuses. Good thing Kitt was not squeamish at the sight of blood—she wouldn't have lasted one fucking week as his girlfriend.

"It was an accident."

Jace lifted his head as Skylar spoke. She had planned on splitting her research between reading police reports and informing the group with each new tidbit of detail she found. "Car wreck, right?" He sat up on the edge of the bed as Kitt wrapped her arms and her legs around him with her chin on his shoulder. "That much, Alex learned before we got here."

Skylar popped a perfectly manicured brow. In all honesty, Jace often wondered if she had help with that via cosmetic wizardry or if the woman just had perfect damn brows. She pivoted in the chair to face them. "Yes, but what is strange is they were the only ones involved in the accident. There was zero trace of other vehicles for miles. They did not hit or were not hit by anyone. The car simply made a sharp right turn while going 70 miles per hour, broke through a guardrail, and landed in the lake."

She spun her laptop around for them to see. "I have a friend that was able to get me access to the traffic cam for that section of the road. Look for yourself." She hit play and a low-quality video began.

Jace moved to his feet and knelt in front of the small table to get a closer look at the grainy footage playing on the laptop screen. Skylar had summed it up rather completely—nothing else was in the lane of traffic and as far as Jace could tell, there were no tell-tale swatches of headlights to show other cars approaching from either direction. "No animals. And it's not a swerve like the Mr. Bishop fell asleep." Hitting rewind, he watched the footage once more. "And look…you can make out the bastard grabbing the wheel and sending them off the road."

Kitt moved to the edge of the bed to join them and shook her head. "But why would he do that?"

Jace looked back over his shoulder at her. "Death wish, perhaps. For him and his wife? A murder/suicide scenario?"

Skylar sat back and chewed on one of her nails. Jace could tell by the way she stared straight ahead, her face tense, that her mind had switched gears for faster mental processing—sorting and discarding as she went. There was a reason she was one of the sharpest paralegals in Texas—if not beyond. She was smart. Damn smart. "The man we just met did not present as someone that wanted to end it." She smirked. "If he is, he needs to take lessons from you, Jace." She circled a finger. "The 'you before you died' you. Not the 'after you died,' you. You know, 'the nuthouse' you."

Kitt gasped and Skylar sharply looked at her and then Jace. "What? Oh please. After everything, including murdering you and bringing you back to life, my calling the psycho place a nut house is shocking? And can we all also come to terms that Jace was like a sad suicidal puppy when we all first met him? Pretty sure we can all agree that being polite flew out the window along with our professional ethics."

Jace's chin hit his chest as he shook his head slowly. "I was not that bad."

His eyes slid up to see both women staring at him and sighed. "Okay, fine. I was that bad. But now, I'm just brooding and devastatingly handsome."

It was that moment Zane chose to enter the conversation. "No. You're just brooding. I'm the handsome one in the Dead Man Crew."

All three of them gawked at Zane and Jace stood up. "Keep telling yourself that, buddy. Maybe one day, a woman will also believe that and you can get laid." He slapped a hand on Zane's shoulder as he walked by and gave Skylar a wink.

Zane sputtered. "I get laid. Dude, women love me. Look at me."

They all stared at him a second time as Zane crossed his arms on his chest, lifted his chin, and then looked away. "I need better friends. Ones that can recognize my awesomeness and my 'boy-next-door' charm."

Skylar started laughing and in doing so, appeared to cause Zane to deflate—much to Jace's amusement. Did Zane actually care for her more than just the playful flirting the two often exhibited? Interesting. Jace was about to ask Zane to step out onto the balcony with him to broach the subject, when the hotel door opened and Franklin and Alex bustled in.

"Hypothermia. That's the only thing that saved her." Franklin stated. He and Alex were apparently in mid-conversation when they walked in. It continued as if the two of them were not aware of the others and still alone.

"But why is she like this now? They followed procedure and from what I can tell, she was warmed gradually, monitored, and should have recovered, Franklin. There was no water left in her lungs after initial emergency triage. She should not be in this vegetative state." Alex's hands animated in motion with each word. The faster the movements, the more determined she became to be correct in the discussion.

"Nor does that explain why she's carving my name in her skin." The two of them halted their speaking to blink at Jace, who lifted a hand to wave hello with a smirk. "So…a car wreck. Without cause. Hypothermia from the cold. And water in her lungs. So, drowning. And yet, she lives." He considered if that would be the correct term to describe the poor woman's state, but none better presented themselves. "Living but yet, not alive. But not 'dead-dead.'" Now Jace sounded like Zane—an idiot.

Kitt snickered as she sat on the table edge near Sky to add, "Live-ish? Dead-ish?"

Zane, ego evidently able to recover quickly, also joined in. "'Dead, but her husband is such an asshole, she had to stick around and watch him suffer,' dead."

Skylar dropped her head down to meet her upraised hands as they came up. "Am I the token nice person in this group? When was I bestowed the honor?" She shoved Kitt off the table. "Go say something sweet and kind. I don't want the title of 'the nice one.' I want the 'badass bitch' role."

Jace couldn't help but chuckle as they all continued, pulling Skylar's laptop with him as he moved to sit on the bed. Playing the video again, he tilted his head to try to see something that the tape had not recorded. Impossible, yes, but he still tried. He could not make out enough of the car to see if there was some demonic, uninvited passenger with the married couple. He slowed it down to see if there was an unexplained shadow on the road, the roof of the car. Anywhere.

And found nothing.

"I need to see her."

The others stopped and turned to regard him. He closed the laptop and was on his feet. "I need to be in the room with her. I can't tell shit through the glass. Can we get me access to her? Just me and this Amanda person?"

Alex twisted the hem of her cardigan in her hand. "I do not think that is a good idea. At all. She has sudden episodes which cannot be explained, nor predicted."

"And she carves my name in her skin." Jace stated plainly.

Franklin removed his round-lensed glasses, which always reminded Jace of John Lennon, and leveled a rare, serious look at Jace. "And her husband is teetering on not letting us help at all. He hasn't said we couldn't, but he's not thrilled to give us a chance. If you cause her to deteriorate or she has a violent reaction, we could lose access altogether."

"And I shall say it again, she carves my name. In. Her. Skin." He crossed his arms and returned the serious look tenfold.

Zane let out a long, overly-dramatic snort. "You keep saying that like it's tee-shirt ready, dude. It so is not. Maybe for the goth crowd, but the marketing for it would be a *bitch*."

CHAPTER SIX

"No."

They approached Mr. Bishop the next morning. To say the man was not in a cooperative mood would be a huge fucking understatement. When Jace and the others arrived, they were informed they were to wait in the lobby. Alex showed them the badge designating her as a visiting professional assigned to the woman's case, but it had zero sway with the nicely attired security staff. Her privileges had been revoked and they were to wait there in the lobby. They sat for close to an hour before Mr. Bishop and his wife's doctor cared to join them. In that time, Jace had not only hit his limit on people-ing skills, but all that remained of his small, designated quantity of daily patience had been exhausted. As Bishop approached, Jace was on his feet and the two of them were in each other's faces. When the man said that word, "no," very simply, as if it would suffice for this bullshit, Jace was a single hair from beating the man's ass.

"Really?" Jace's lip curled up off his teeth in a sneer and he refused to be the one to blink as he and Bishop engaged in a cavemen-level, alpha-male stare-down. "I am here to help your wife." Each word following coated with sarcasm. "Do you want her to just die like you wanted her to when you drove the fucking car into the lake?" Sure, it was a low-blow and Jace was not entirely sure of its accuracy. But something felt way off and he was determined to find out what. And, to be honest with himself, if Laura's demon had found a new host? He damn sure wanted a second chance at that bitch.

Bishop pushed him back and the others rushed forward to tug Jace away before a fist fight broke out in the posh nuthouse lobby. Jace jerked as he fought a fight instinct but kept the distance between him and Bishop. "Look, I get it. You're not sure what is going on. Or who I am. Or why I'm here. I'd fucking *love* to answer those questions, but I can't do that without knowing *why* your wife is carving *my* name on her own skin. If you can answer that for me, sure, I'll leave right now. Back to the warm and sun and not this damn wet ass, chilly Ohio weather." Jace knew how the man felt—threatened and scared, so he put his hand out for the man to shake. "Prove me wrong that you give a shit about your wife and let's get the answers."

Bishop rejected the offer of Jace's handshake and instead, opted to further violate Jace's personal space. "Fine. You can see her once and then you go. Understood?" Jace took the opportunity to search Bishop's eyes for any demonic clue. No such luck. Bishop, in a total male move, shoved Jace and put a finger in his face. That was Jace's signature move—he would consider this a learning opportunity to know what it felt like to be on the receiving end of it. But he'd still do it, regardless. "Are we clear, Camden?"

Jace gave the man his best bullshitting smile as his hand dropped to his side. "Clear as a bell." That is, if that bell were in fog. Under the Gulf of Mexico. Wrapped in a towel… clear.

The others waited on the observation side of the glass. Dr. Lewis stood at the keypad and paused before he keyed in the code to give Jace access to Amanda Bishop. "I should tell you now, she has given zero response to anyone who has tried to elicit one. Not me, the staff, nor her husband. I am afraid you are going to be greatly disappointed, Mr. Camden."

"It's okay, Doc. I'm rather used to disappointment." Jace's focus was on the woman who sat beyond the door and glass, restrained to her wheelchair. Even from here, he could make out the healing rows of cuts and scratches. A few showed letters of his name. That creeped Jace out more than he cared to admit.

"Mr. Camden? Do you understand?"

His eyes skidded over to Dr. Lewis. "Yeah, yeah. Let's see if you're right. I hope I get a shit load of disappointment and she does nada, which means I go home." He gave the man a tight smile. "And yes, I understand."

Dr. Lewis did not appear convinced, but proceeded to tap in the code anyway. The beeping of it being entered sounded harsher to Jace's ears than it should, as the lock disengaged. Jace stepped inside and fought down his own claustrophobic fears when the door locked—leaving him just as much a prisoner as the patient. Remaining close to the room's entryway, he went down on his haunches to observe Amanda Bishop. He waited to see if she reacted to his presence but no, she didn't even twitch.

Jace was glad she was clean—most likely this place gave one hell of a sponge bath. It gave him some comfort that the staff cared for the woman, even if her husband did not. Her hair was pulled back in a ponytail and even in this state, he could tell she was pretty. His eyes trailed to the healing scars and landed on her wedding band. Turning his head, he stared at the glass for a few seconds. Did Bishop wear a matching one? For the life of him, Jace could not recall if he did. It shouldn't be too surprising, but most removed their symbols of marriage *after* their loved one had passed. Some, like Jace, hung on to it long after.

Doctor Lewis' words came to mind. But whether Steven believed it or not, Amanda Bishop was not dead. Not yet.

Her chest moved slightly with shallow breathing. The drool that ran from her dry, cracked lips attested to her living status—at least in regard to her body. Standing slowly, as if she would vanish or startle, Jace walked forward and slowly placed one hand and then the other on the padded armrests of the wheelchair. "Amanda, you wanted to see me? I'm here. So, show me you are too."

"I don't like this." Kitt was chewing on her index fingernail as she watched through the glass. Jace was not the only one that felt odd and off since arriving in Ohio. Maybe it could be attributed to the fact she was not a traveler. She, like Amanda Bishop, considered herself a total homebody. But a queasy, gut-twisted feeling had settled in the moment the airplane had touched down. Glancing sideways as Skylar linked their arms together, Kitt's eyes swung back to watch Jace try to elicit something…anything from the woman in the room beyond. "And before you ask why, I got zilch. I just don't like any of this. Wish I knew." She pointed to her boyfriend. "I just always feel so helpless. Like once again, he has to do this weirdo, bizarro stuff alone."

Skylar nodded as she replied, "But at least we didn't have to kill him this time." Then she let out a nervous short laugh. "Yet."

"Excuse me?" The doctor squeaked. Both he and the woman's husband had overheard. Kitt couldn't help but laugh.

Skylar answered by showing both men her most charming smile. "Inside joke between my friend, Kitt and me. We don't *really* kill him." Skylar then whispered for only Kitt to hear. "He kills himself. A totally different experience." She followed that fact with a playful wink.

God, it was so twisted that they could joke about what had happened. Kitt knew she was the last to join into that humor and maybe would have joined in this time as well. But that twisting in her gut had not abated, even if her mood had. Skylar kept her arm linked with Kitt's in understanding support as they both returned to observing Jace.

Franklin and Alexis stood to the left with Mr. Bishop and Dr. Lewis to the right. The physician chewed on his bottom lip anxiously, but Kitt found Mr. Bishop's features held a strange expression. Was it glee? That seemed highly unlikely considering the circumstances. She must be reading him wrong. Focusing back on the activity beyond the glass, she put her palm against it and whispered, "Be careful, baby."

Jace wasn't sure if the woman in her comatose state registered his presence at all. With a sigh, he gave the mirror a sideways glance before he moved closer to squat directly in front of the wheelchair. Her eyes were vacant and appeared feverish. The doctors had said nothing about her having an illness beyond a trapped mind within the shell of Amanda Bishop. His previous comparison of her being like a fluttering butterfly trapped in a too small box seemed more accurate up close. Its wings becoming more frayed and damaged with each crash into its prison's sides. The longer she remained trapped, the more unseen damage she took. Eventually, she wouldn't be able to fly at all. Jace reached out to touch her knee. "Amanda, why are you carving my name in your flesh? Can you answer me?"

A minute went by and Jace sat there motionless with his touch on Amanda's knee. Seconds ticked by and he considered giving up.

Until he sensed *something* had joined them.

And it was not Amanda who answered back.

Its calling card Jace knew all too well. He heard, then watched as black frost crackled and spread over the mirror in front of the others. His breath misted in seconds. The frantic banging of fists on the other side of the glass and muted screams of alarm from Kitt beyond gave Jace clear and undeniable signs. This was not a psychotic snap taking place only in Jace's head.

He knew better now. It never had been. Not as a child or as an adult, when he was written off as insane.

The demons had found a new way to get to him.

And Amanda Bishop started to laugh.

A twisted, demonic, cold inhuman voice sounded from her lips, though her face remained stone blank as before. Her mouth became unnaturally animated as it hissed out two spine-freezing words, "Hello, Jace."

Jace steeled himself not to scramble back in fear. To not show whatever demon was controlling the poor woman's body that he wanted to run out of the room. He had survived fighting the soul-sucker attached to Laura. He had gone to death, beyond, and back. It was not a trip Jace planned on taking again. Hell, he'd willingly get on a million airplanes aka mass death coffins before going through that any time soon. He licked his suddenly dry lips and moved closer. That led to fighting the nausea that stirred his stomach, the headache that crept into his brain, and the tickle of a nose-bleed in his sinuses. He would not fucking back down from this or any demon.

"Oh goody, you know my first name too. Yay, me." He smiled sardonically and narrowed his eyes. "Something tells me you're a different one. Not the same demon bitch from before, right? Figures, she doesn't have the balls to show her ugly demon face to me. That is, if your kind has genders."

Amanda, or more precisely, the demon controlling her, laughed again. "We have no *he* or *she*. We only have *us*. And we are going to have *you*. We've waited too fucking long."

"What is happening?!"

Doctor Miller lost his shit and Kitt would have thought Mr. Bishop had more than enough reason to react in the same way. But she would have been wrong. He looked almost disinterested in the black frost as it spread across the mirror. It quickly obscured their view of what took place in the room beyond between Jace and Mrs. Bishop within seconds. Skylar and Zane were beating on the glass and Franklin was trying to wrench the door open, while Alex ran to get help.

Franklin hauled Dr. Miller, who tried to cower in the corner, over to the door. "Open it! Now!"

The doctor tried to key in the code only to hiss, jerk back his hand, and step backwards in horror. "It's frozen. How is it frozen?!"

Franklin shoved him away, jerked his amulet free from its cord from his shirt and touched it to the ice-covered lock. The amulet sizzled and water dripped, as the icy build-up started to melt. But more instantly accumulated behind the knob and panel preventing it from being of any use. Franklin started kicking the door and yelled an answer to the panicked doctor the man had not been prepared to hear. "Demons, Doctor Miller. What you are seeing are demons. And we just gave them someone they have wanted for a very long time."

Kitt put both of her hands on the frozen glass and closed her eyes. "Draw a door. Draw a door." She pleaded in hopes Jace would not only hear her, but feel her nearby, as tears ran down her cheek. It was warm and then turned icy when it hit her bare forearm. "Please, baby, find me. Draw a fucking door and get back to me."

Amanda ripped through the restraints faster than Jace could move back. She let out a high-pitched shriek as she attacked and sent them both to the floor. Jace held her up above him and tried his best not to hurt the woman, while trying to keep the demon possessing her from eating his fucking face. She clawed at his arms and snapped her teeth with her eyes rolled back so far in her head, only the whites showed. Throwing her off, Jace got to his feet and dared a glance at the door, when he heard something striking it—pounding sounds louder from behind the glass. The last thing he wanted was for this demon to get out of this room to where Kitt and the others were. Educated from his most recent battle, Jace knew the demons would stop at nothing to break him down, including trying to kill the woman he loved and his friends. He needed to keep this demon contained, end it, and also survive. Bent at the waist, he smiled. "Well, here I am. Let's get to know each other."

The demon screamed and Amanda's body jerked in an odd "tethered by invisible strings" way. Perhaps the demon had not perfected the bond with its human puppet yet. When it ran at Jace, he had been able to side-step the move easily and let it crash into a wall. It let out a frustrated hiss, spun around, and came at him again. Jace pivoted, but the wheelchair came flying at him, hitting him in the chest and sent him crashing to the floor. The demon adapted how it used Amanda's body and its own supernatural powers with astonishing quickness, unfortunately for Jace. He rolled to his back and the demon was on him as it started laughing. A hand went up and then down to punch him in the chest over his heart. Demon Amanda came in low and snarled in his face, thick strands of drool dripping from her tongue and teeth. "We were told you have a little problem, warrior. One of the heart."

Jace's eyes went wide as the demon's fingers splayed out and pain shot through him from the touch. His heart did a staggered beat and tried to regulate only to fail. Jace let out an angry growl and wrapped his hand around Amanda's thin wrist as he struggled in vain. The demon actually smiled as his heart beat once. The next beat came seconds behind the first and after what seemed like an eternity, thumped with a third. Cold crackled through him and his teeth chattered from the chill. This too, Jace had experienced before—a bitch element, really. He was starting to realize that having a learn-as-we-go mentality about all of this had been a mistake. But it was too late to change that path now. He guessed he and the demons would find out together.

Alex rushed back into the observation room with an armed security guard and a very large male nurse. Kitt pointed to the glass. "We have to get in there! It's been too long!"

Both men seemed confused, shock clear on their faces as they took in the scene, but the security guard recovered first. "Step back, ma'am."

Kitt took several steps from the window and the others followed suit. The guard lifted a chair and swung it. Cracks appeared in the mirror and the chair arced once more. Deeper, wider cracks appeared in the glass, as the black frost began to seep from, dripping down the surface before splattering on the floor. It melted instantly as it struck. The third chair strike shattered it and a rush of unnatural, foul, frigid air came from inside the padded room. Kitt scrambled over the window opening, giving no notice to the sharp, tiny squares of tempered glass. "Jace! Baby!"

She found him lying on the floor with the Bishop woman curled up next to him. Both she and Jace were pale, which sent her fear skyward. Kitt went to her knees next to Jace as she touched his face. He was cold—icy cold. She screamed at Franklin. "He's inside. He's somewhere inside!"

The nurse rushed over with Alex to check Jace's vitals. "There's no pulse. No breathing." The man yelled back at Doctor Lewis, who stayed cowering in the observation area. "Get some help in here! He's coded." The nurse firmly pushed Kitt back as he started CPR, but she remained on Jace's opposite side, holding his hand, desperately whispering under her breath, "I'm here, baby. Find me. Please find me."

Jace heard Kitt and he hated hearing the desperate tone in her voice. "Talk about déjà vu," he mumbled under his breath. He found himself standing in the middle of road. It was obviously night but there were zero stars. Only darkness, pavement, and double-yellow lines. It was cold with frost lining the edges of the roadway, but not the usual nature-generated kind—this frost was black. "Great."

When he had gone inside of Laura's nightmare realm with the demons, it had been the room she had died in—their bedroom, after a fight. He assumed this was where Amanda Bishop's soul was trapped. Looking around them, he had no fucking idea how he was supposed to find a door here in the middle of vast nothing, but perhaps time would tell. How much? Who knew? He sure as hell didn't. His heart must have stopped--that Jace was sure of. If the others were able to bring him back without any preparations? Yep, toss that into the "no idea" bucket with the rest. He had taken two steps, when a light appeared in front of him. Narrowing his eyes, it came closer at a supernatural rate. One minute, a pinpoint of light miles away and in the next, a speeding car's headlights. It came straight for him. He jumped to the side seconds too late, but the car went *through* him rather than crashing into him. It then skittered as if they had collided, swerved, and went over the embankment to hit the shore of the lake at the side of the road.

Jace stared at the wreckage in bewilderment as he recovered and rose to his feet. He ran to the slope, climbed down, and found the car on its passenger side with half the vehicle already submerged. He attempted to grab the door handle, but his hand went through it. He was nothing more than a ghost, trying to prove he still had substance. Here, in the burnt in memories of when Amanda Bishop's soul became…

Well, Jace wasn't sure really.

Stuck? Hung? No idea. But he felt without a doubt that this was that unnamed moment.

Cupping his hands on the cracked car window, Jace could see that Amanda Bishop was obviously unconscious, yet he could not see any real injury. There was no blood. She had landed slumped sideways and the water overtook her as it intruded the car. Seeing movement, Jace stepped back as her husband climbed out of the busted windshield to exit the wreckage. The man did not even give a backwards glance. No assistance. He did not even call out to his wife.

"What the fuck? Hey! Hey!" Bishop could have easily gotten Amanda out of the seat belt and pulled her through the opening he had just used to exit. But the man did nothing to come to the aid of the now hurt and drowning woman.

"You sonofabitch! Do something!" Jace followed Steven through the water, carrying a rage of disbelief with him as he approached the man on the highway. Bishop stood there, staring at the car and not doing a thing. Jace gave the man a moment of credit—perhaps he suffered from shock? But no, he could see that Bishop's eyes were focused. Perhaps even calculating?

Jace stepped right in front of him, even if Bishop couldn't feel or see him, and roared, "Why aren't you helping your wife!?"

"We have a pulse. Everyone back up."

Kitt went weak with relief, letting her head drop to Jace's chest to feel it rise and fall. Color began flushing his skin and she wanted nothing more than to get him to an airplane the very second he came to and take him home. Even if she had to use Amanda's tipped over wheelchair to get him there. Back to the beach he loved. In the Texas warmth and the salty air. Away from this toxic place and she had no idea how to quantify why…she just knew it.

Alex and Franklin spoke with the doctor and nurse. She overheard them state Jace had a heart problem but had been stable. She turned her head to see the Bishop woman lying there, still curled up with vacant eyes surrounded by a slack featured face and pale skin. But then, right before Kitt looked away, in a blink, she could have sworn Amanda's eyes focused on her. Was there a small, slight smile touching her lips? Or did she imagine that?

Kitt swallowed as she trained her eyes on Amanda to see if it would happen again. No, the woman was still in the same comatose state as before. Kitt glanced back as she protected Jace to find Bishop has *finally* lost his strange cool.

"Get the fuck away from me!" Bishop jerked Franklin's hand from his arm, apparently pissed the druid dared to invade his personal space. "I want you people *out* of here. Away from my wife! What did he do to her?" He then grabbed Doctor Lewis and pinned the man aggressively into the corner. Dr. Lewis seemed to be in shock with little reaction other than eyes blinking behind thick glasses.

"Kitt, let Zane and I get Jace off the floor. He should be coming back any minute." Franklin moved back to Jace and Kitt desperately sought calm in the older man's eyes. A calm she had a very hard time finding. Of course, Franklin did not let her down and she let out shaky breath with a nod. Getting to her feet, she moved far away enough for Franklin and Zane to situate Jace on a gurney that had been wheeled in. Holding his hand, she kissed the back of it and continued to whisper the phrase, "I'm here, baby. Come back to me." Jace had come to once and said he heard her calling to him on the realm. With or without a pulse.

The nurse continued to monitor Jace's vitals and nodded to Kitt in encouragement. More medical personnel entered to lift Amanda and settle her back in the wheelchair and check her condition. Kitt could not stop herself from watching for some sign Amanda had changed, like before. But just as before, Kitt received no validation.

"Kitt, look."

Alex had taken up a place at the opposite side of the gurney and was pointing at Jace's arm. Kitt glanced down in confusion and then became alarmed. Words were carved in his flesh just like the type that had appeared in the Bishop woman's flesh. But it was not Jace's name. Not even close. Just two words…

No Help.

"Shh, take it easy. Go slow, Jace."

He sat up, startled, and blinked in a useless attempt to clear his fuzzy mind and plot his disconnected thoughts. Skylar's face came into view as the others stood by near the hotel room table. "He was no help," Jace croaked out. They had all turned to stare at him and Kitt moved to sit next to him on the bed.

"Well, that explains your special little note."

Jace looked at Skylar in confusion and then glanced down, when her fingers tapped on his forearm. And by "note," she meant the bloody words scratched onto his arm. What they meant; he had no idea. He looked at the words and wondered; was Amanda is the one calling him out and not the demons?

He rolled off the bed to stand, but instantly became woozy and his ass dropped back down to sit on the edge. "What happened? While I was in?"

Franklin moved closer and brought a cool hand to lay on Jace's neck. "You died. Your heart stopped when the episode inside the room escalated. The usual sign of the black frost made an appearance, but we were obscured from seeing what actually occurred on your side. Even the monitoring cameras were coated and unable to record. We had to break the glass and found both you and Mrs. Bishop laying on the floor. She, in her former comatose state, and you coded."

Jace's fingers gripped the edge of the mattress as he attempted to get his brain to kick-start. "Coded, as in died? As in died *again*?" The obvious answer did not need to be said aloud. It was reflected on each face and he hissed out, "shit," through his teeth before he succeeded in standing. Less dizzy by the second, they explained how it was demanded he be brought back to the hotel to recover. Jace looked down at Kitt and found her features awash with concern.

"I doubted you would have liked to come to there and the place was in panic mode after what happened. They were talking about locking it down. I did not want you there. Alex convinced them to let you go after she explained you had," her hand reached up to splay over his chest, "a heart condition."

"Not that it matters." Franklin added, head down to clean his glasses. Jace guessed the lenses were already spotless before the process, a sign the man was stressed and needed an outlet for that negative energy. "We are not allowed to set foot in the facility. Mr. Bishop's words were filled with rage, but the strange thing was he seemed cool, almost overly calculating prior to their delivery.

Franklin's glasses were slid on and he met Jace's eyes. "The husband is not at all what he seems. But I picked up no other energy from him. And the amulet had zero reaction when I touched it to him." He shrugged and let out a heavy sigh. "In the shuffle, I wanted to determine if we dealt with an evil supernatural element to Mr. Bishop we were unable to see. But no. The amulet did not react."

Zane laughed and slapped Franklin on the back. "Look at you, Frankie! Going all badass ninja druid in the middle of a fight. I'm impressed."

Franklin responded with a sheepish smile and a glance over to Alex. Perhaps to see if his actions had made a heroic impression on her too. Jace would add that strange interaction to a long list of confusing developments amongst his friends to figure out once they returned home. But for now, he had to get them all home.

Jace frowned and put his head back to fill in details with more thought as his mind cleared. "Doesn't matter. I saw the wreck. She's trapped. And was trapped then. Somehow," he brought his head forward to regard each of them, "her soul is between death and here. I just don't know how the fuck to correct that. Or which side she'll be on if I do."

Zane had begun to eat his way through a can of Pringles, his fidget tell—nervous snacking. The man's eyes went wide, mouth formed an "O" complete with half-chewed chips and he spoke around the bite, "So, what you're saying is we're making shit up as we go just like the last time?"

Jace nodded and Zane swallowed a mouthful of chips and pointed at him with the now empty can. "Now, see. *That* is t-shirt material."

Skylar quickly jerked the can from his grasp and hit him in the head with it. She looked at the others smugly. "What? It made *me* feel better."

CHAPTER SEVEN

"You have got to be kidding me." Kitt expressed what all of them likely wanted to say at the news that Bishop did not even try to save his wife. He had also made it clear their help was unwanted—the ruse of pretending it was no longer necessary.

Four of them sat inside the small coffee shop a few blocks from the mental facility with a view of Lake Erie at the end of the street where they were discussing next steps. In spite of the warning from Mr. Bishop to stay away from Amanda, they had attempted again that morning. But only Alexis and Franklin were allowed in as a matter of professional courtesy. It had been granted in order to speak to Dr. Lewis in regards to what was being called "the incident". Shit, if incidents were wanted, Jace had a long list for discussion. It would have occupied Mrs. Bishop's medical staff for days-and-days. But after being told how Amanda's chief physician had behaved during the last one—a list would not be needed. Sounded like just the one had been too much for Dr. Lewis to deal with.

Jace had been able to tell them more about what he had seen in the woman's nightmare realm, once he had gotten some sleep. Skylar soaked it in like an intellectual sponge. Zane nodded with his mouth busy with two different types of donuts and a bagel. Skylar nibbled on a scone while downing her third cup of coffee.

Jace's eyes kept sliding sideways to Kitt, who sat next to him in the booth where she nursed a green tea and waved off ordering any food. She said her nerves had her stomach messed up and she wasn't hungry. He was worried about her and did his best not to give power to the negative places that his mind wanted to go. This must be wearing on her emotions and her appetite paid the price of the toll. There weren't many girlfriends that could handle having their boyfriend die not only once, but twice in the span of so many months. He squeezed his hand on her thigh, kissed her jaw, and she rested her head on his shoulder before he continued. "Bishop didn't do a damn thing. The car went into the ditch and he just stood there."

Skylar was taking actual notes on her laptop and her hazel eyes came up to meet Jace's, that sharp-edged paralegal mode firmly in place. "It may have nothing to do with anything supernatural. It would not be the first case of an unhappy husband. Maybe their marriage was on the rocks. Or he was cheating." She turned her laptop around to show them. "His Facebook profile, as well as hers, is set to public posting. They look happy. Lots of couple pictures. Vacation shots, arm-in-arm. An unbelievably cute dog that sonofabitch doesn't deserve. I mean," she clicked on a picture of some purebred small-sized dog, "look at that furry face! It's so cute. Yes you are. Such a good, cute doggie."

She realized she had gone into baby-speak out loud at the image of the pet, flipped them all off the bird finger, and turned the device back around with the legal eagle façade snapped firmly into place. "But again, murderers have cute pets and positive social media as well. From what I can tell, they gave no indication…" She paused, leaned in, and narrowed her eyes. "Wait a minute. They had tried IVF. Mrs. Bishop says they had their third and last round of IVF a few months ago. They were giving up and coping with the idea of not having children naturally. That shit is not cheap. But other than a sad face and that status, it's the only sign that not all was happy, joy-joy in Bishop marriageland."

Zane chewed and pointed from his place next to Skylar. "That's rough. But he also wouldn't be the first dude that fell out of love because he couldn't have a kid. You ever watched Game of Thrones? It's all about having a son. To carry on the name. Judging by Bishop's bastard mentality, he's old school about all of that. Adopting some deserving kid, not even an option. Blood or nothing with his type." He sat back and sighed. "As a kid that found a home through adoption, I am not a real fan of that kind of person."

Skylar looked over at Zane, sharply in shock. "You were adopted? Really?" Jace noticed a rare tender softness flash in her eyes as she asked.

"Yeah. I was in the system from birth to twelve-years old. Then got adopted by a nice older couple." Zane became uncomfortable with the personal subject matter about himself and his eyes darted around the coffee shop. "I'm going to get another doughnut." He then stood up to make his way through the crowded shop.

Both Jace and Skylar's eyes went to the untouched remaining doughnut and they met gazes. Zane never just stopped eating and forgot a doughnut. Jace sat forward and asked Sky quietly, "Did you know any of that?"

Skylar shook her head. "No. I don't think I ever asked. I know his parents died a few years ago, but I had no idea he was a foster and then adopted."

Jace pivoted to track Zane and sighed. "I didn't either. He never really talked about it. And well, with my rule of not talking about *my* past for so long…" Turning back, he slowly wadded a paper napkin in his fingers. "Damn, I feel like a pretty crappy friend right now."

Skylar snorted. "Because you are. You were. And you always will be." But she gave him an understanding smile before returning her focus to the laptop. "But we love you anyway. We need gold stars. Medals. Combat pay. T-shirts."

Zane had shown back up and perked up. "T-shirts? Are we back on that subject?" He slid back into the booth with the easy-going smile back in place. "I have ideas."

"She's back in her comatose state. We tried to tell them that you did not release her from the wheelchair, but without video evidence or a witness to the event, our words fell on deaf ears. They also accused you of tampering with the sprinkler system to explain away the water in the room. Bishop said he's having his wife discharged and moved home in a week. The word, "hospice" was tossed into our faces with enough venom to sour the sweetest of advice. We are at an impasse, I'm afraid." Alex was chewing on her nail as she filled them in. Both she and Franklin had joined them at the hotel room after speaking with Mrs. Bishop's medical staff. "He said he will forego the restraining order if you stay away. However," she added a second fingernail to her chewing tactic, "he said he will speak with you. Alone. Away from the hospital and without any of us." She lowered her hands to her lap and clasped them together in a manner to compose herself as she met Jace's eyes. "We told him no. Of course."

Jace frowned. "Tell him yes. I want that bastard. Something does not make sense." He moved away and crossed his arms as his eyes went downcast to the floor. "If he's human and Amanda is the one a demon has attached itself to, why does he not care? I don't need to be near her to find out now that I have been given access to her nightmare state, but I need to know how she got to this point. And he's the key to that. She most likely has no fucking idea." He lifted his head with a nod. "Yeah, tell him it's a go. I'll meet with him."

Kitt stepped in front of him. "Hey. No. That's almost as stupid a decision as some of the others you've made. We don't do this alone anymore." She brought her hands up to cup his face and looked deep into his eyes. Jace found concern, worry, and a touch of anger at him for putting them in this situation to begin with.

"You have to agree that this Bishop guy, he's nuts. Crazy. Let me go with you. Or Zane. Heck, Skylar can kick him in the nuts or say she's your legal counsel. Baby, please, don't do this alone." She leaned forward to rest her forehead on his chest and whispered, "I know you're going to, but I am hoping, for once, you'll do what I want you to."

Jace wrapped his arms around her and tilted her chin up to meet his eyes. "I can't. Not this time. I'm sorry, but I hear you. I won't do any hero shit. Promise."

Kitt yanked her chin from his hold angrily. "Right. Like you promised not to die again. What did it take? One whole day for that to be broken. Whatever, Jace, do what you are going to do. You always do." She then stalked away to the bathroom and added a slammed door for emphasis.

Jace stared at the door, his jaw dropped, and glanced at the others. They shifted awkwardly, followed with cleared throats as if they had not seen the emotional outburst. Sure, Kitt had been put through the wringer when they released Laura from the demon that fed on her soul, but even then she hadn't behaved this quick-tempered. Shrugging, he went to the door and knocked as he brought his head close to the door, keeping his voice low. "Kitt, come on. What do you expect me to do here? Tell me. I'm listening."

The door came flying open and it was obvious she had been crying. She came into his personal space, inches from his face and simply said, "Go home. Now. With me."

Jace felt helpless in the onslaught of her pleading—the desperation pouring off her like waves to crash against his still-recovering senses. "Kitt, if I do that, this woman, Amanda Bishop is as good as dead. You heard Franklin and Alex. He's going to put her in hospice and let her die."

Kitt's face flushed with frustrated anger. "Good. Let her. Better than you."

CHAPTER EIGHT

Jace had tried to reach an understanding with Kitt, but she was as stubborn as he was. Normally, he loved that about her, but not in this situation. Skylar had arranged the meeting with Mr. Bishop and the best location they could come to an agreement on was a part of the city on the lake's edge. Bishop had demanded one of the covered picnic areas at the farthest point from the parking lot. Hard-honed defensive instincts had Jace on edge about how this could go down. If Bishop tried anything, he would have to tap into the fighting "toolbox" he had gladly put away months ago after Laura moved on. Sure, he still ran and even worked out at the gym but going toe-to-toe with an adversary? Nope. Calculate the supernatural strength of a demon that may or may not come into play on Bishop's side, odds were not good in Jace's favor.

Sitting on the table, Jace pulled his coat around him as a cold breeze whipped off the water on the lake when a dark Mercedes pulled up and Bishop vacated the vehicle via the driver's side. At least the man had kept their agreement to come alone. It put them on equal ground in that aspect. Jace did, however, wish he had taken Skylar's advice to record the encounter.

Bishop spotted Jace as he moved to his feet and both men stood there measuring each other up. Jace did not budge as Bishop approached and he knew better than to hold a hand out. He was pretty sure it would be rejected once again or slapped away. Steven Bishop looked pissed already and not a single word had been uttered yet.

"I did some research on you, Camden." Bishop spoke to him, not bothering with pleasantries any more than Jace did, as he approached the shelter. "You have quite the record. Arrested for murder. Got away with it. Assaults. Got away with a few of those. Did probation for others. In and out of nut houses like they were outlet malls. What I didn't learn…" He had reached Jace and now stood a yard away to sneer with obvious contempt. "Is why my wife knew you. Or why you are here. You're not a doctor. Not a shrink. Just some guy who used his dead wife's money to take other people's fucking money in the name of charity."

Jace snorted and added an exaggerated, dramatic eyeroll. "Oh goody. You Googled me. I might be a little bit flattered. But all that is public record, bud. And has zero to do with why I'm here." Jace resumed his seat on the corner of the table and cocked his head to the side. "Which you must be curious about or you wouldn't have wanted to have this little chitty-chat. But I have one question, Bishop." He gave the man a cold smile. "Why didn't you help your wife at the wreck? You climbed out, you stood there, and you were going to let her drown. I have to wonder what kind of husband does that?"

Bishop's shocked surprise was so great, the man didn't stand a chance in hell hiding it. However, Jace was slightly amused to watch the man try. First there was confusion, check. Then there was anger, also check. Easy to register as the man's cheeks grew ruddy with color. After all, none of that had been in the police records Skylar had received. Only that Steven Bishop was found sitting by the car and the police statement stated he appeared frantic that his wife remained in the car. The authorities chalked up the man's lack of action to save his wife to the trauma of the accident.

Jace pushed up to step forward and met Bishop's gaze. "Why did you want your wife dead? And why do you still want that?" He slowly smiled and searched Bishop's behavior for any trace of a demon. "What can she possibly do to you now? Or maybe, it's what she can do if she recovers, right, Steven?"

Bishop's slack-jawed mouth was able to sputter, eyes darting around as if this was some sick prank before skidding back to meet Jace's. "What? No. How could you?…" Bishop must have realized he had just confessed to a man he believed stood in the way of his planned ending of a deadly scheme. The man's rage took control to detour the slip-up and he brought his hands up to grab Jace's jacket to jerk him even closer. "Shut up. You're wrong. I love my wife. I tried to help. I couldn't."

Jace, unflustered by the man's escalated emotions, shrugged within Bishop's hold. "I only know what I saw. Because Amanda wanted me to see. Want to know why I'm here?" Jace leaned closer and whispered, "Because you were no help then. You are no help now. She wanted me here to be the help you aren't."

The expected fist sent flying towards Jace's face was halted within inches from it when he caught it in his palm. Bishop's opposite fist was also anticipated and Jace twisted at the waist to avoid it. Bishop let out a roar of anger and Jace pivoted and swept the man's feet out from under him when Bishop failed to tackle Jace.

"Why do you want her dead? Divorce too much of a hassle?"

Bishop let out more angry sounds as he rose to his feet and Jace avoided another attempt to physically engage to fight. Bishop hit the table and was forced to bend over it, looking back over his shoulder. "You don't know what you're talking about. I *love* my wife!"

Bishop pushed off the table and made another move, but this time was able to grab Jace's jacket and land a punch. Jace's chin snapped to the side as he took a step back, but he was able to dodge another and he countered with a fist landing in Bishop's stomach. The impact so hard, the man doubled over from the force of it.

Jace leaned down to snarl in the man's face, "Bullshit. A man that loves a woman doesn't leave her in a ditch to fucking drown." Pushed him away and didn't give a shit when Bishop collapsed to his knees on the ground. For all Jace cared, the fucker could die from exposure—it would give Jace faith in karma if he did. "When a husband loves a wife, they do *anything* they can to save them. Heaven, hell, even fucking death doesn't stop him."

Jace spit out a mouthful of blood and wiped his split lip. "Trust me on the subject." He turned to walk back to the rental car without a backwards glance. "I know it all too well."

"Oh shit, he hit you?" Skylar was examining Jace jaw where a bruise had bloomed over a split lip. Jace pulled way and noticed Kitt was not in the hotel room with them. Skylar sighed and pointed to the door that adjoined the two suites. "She hasn't said a word since you left. She hasn't even come out of the room. And do you want me to contact my peeps on the force to file charges? Did he hit you first?"

Jace waved her off dismissively. "He tried to hit me a few times. He got one punch in and yes, I made sure it was the first." Walking over to the door, he tried the knob and found it locked and he let his forehead hit the wood. "Damn it." He had no more answers than he had before. As satisfying has it had been to see Bishop's aloofness crack, the mystery of what was really going on was no clearer than the mud it had been before. Baffling, supernatural, sticky mud.

"I'm going to have to go under."

He turned to face Alexis, Zane, Skylar and Franklin. "I have to see what I'm missing. What I'm not seeing. And what the Bishops may or may not be. Alex, did you bring…"

"What?"

Kitt's voice behind his back, the door apparently no longer locked and now open. The shrill in her tone told Jace that she had heard his next part of the plan. The accompanying sheepish looks on the other's expressions validated the fact. "Kitt…" He turned to face her to once again try to appease and explain. For him to feel like shit that he made her cry.

Kitt crossed her arms, lifted her chin, and this time, there was not a tear in sight. "If you do that, I'm leaving. I can't do this. Not again. I won't do this. Do you hear me?" Her tone was hard, but Jace could see her bottom lip tremble slightly with each word spoken. "I won't stand by and let you do this for someone you don't even know! You either go home with me today…or I go home alone."

Jace sighed and tried to take her hand but that was a complete no-go. "Kitt, I know you're worried. Even scared. But we knew that we'd have to learn more about this soul warrior gig. And we both knew when we completed freeing Laura, it might not be the end of all of it. Please, baby, just listen…"

But rather do what Jace expected, she took a step back and brought a finger up to point in his face. "No. I can't do this. Not again." Skylar moved forward in an effort to assist with her best friend, but that infamous Kitt Thomas stubborn streak was fully engaged even with her bestie. "You may not mean what you say, Jace. But I do." She jerked her arm away from his hand as he tried to stop her, snagged her jacket and purse, and left.

Jace closed his eyes as Skylar went running after Kitt. Zane let out a whistle and it was not surprising when Sky came back alone. "She grabbed a cab. I couldn't catch her. Jace, maybe she's right. This might be one you should walk away from."

His eyes still closed, he very seriously considered agreeing with her. It would be easy to go back to Galveston and forget Amanda Bishop and her asshole of a husband. Kitt was far more important to Jace than a woman and a marriage he had no invested emotions in. Opening his eyes to find them all waiting to see the next move, he nodded. "Yeah, find out the next flight home. We're not wanted here." He then turned away and entered the empty suite he had shared with Kitt just moments ago. "I just need to lay down." Pointed a finger to his head as he closed the door behind him and left them to make arrangements.

"You can't go. Please."

One moment, Jace was faceplanted in the pillow to sleep after Alex told him there wasn't a flight until the morning and the next, he stood in the middle of that strange highway with Amanda Bishop standing in front of him. Looking to the side and back, he brought his eyes to hers. She appeared vibrantly alive and coherent. Apparently, the connection they had formed previously was still very much connected here, even with miles to separate their physical forms.

"Why? Tell me why I have to stay. I have no idea what the fuck I'm doing."

She gave him a smile. "I know. But there's more to it. You just have to find it all. They said you'd never come. They whisper your name. They say you can save me. Or you can help me go." She wrapped her arms around him as a stab of freezing cold went through him. She was more dead than alive, more proof that for some reason, her soul could not move on. "They said you'd never come. I knew you would come. They whisper your name. Help me or help me come back."

Amanda's vibrant coherency began to disintegrate as she began to babble her last statement over and over. Jace reached up to unwrap her arms from him, but they began to tighten. "Hey, wait…" But as he said the words, Amanda's hold continued to increase until he felt like his ribs would crack. He fought her hold and she started laughing. It was a low, sinister sound and Jace noticed something rushing at them as he struggled. It was dark, like a wave of water, yet writhing with something under the surface. It came crashing towards them and he could make out that it wasn't water at all. The substance wasn't under the surface. It composed the liquid mass. And it seemed to have a million red, piercing eyes, flashing fangs, and claws twisting within it. His mind grasped with horror, it was dozens, if not hundreds of demons and they were coming straight for him and this version of Amanda.

Rearing back a fist and hating what he was about to do, he hit the manifestation in the temple and had to do it a second time for her hold to lessen. Stumbling back, Jace shoved her away and her humanoid form dissolved into one of the soul demons he had fought in the past. He kicked it in the chest and spun around just in time to face the wave of hungry mass of demons. They were three or so yards away and he threw out both his arms and yelled, "Stop!"

And much to his surprise, they did as he commanded. Not only that, but the one that had impersonated Amanda cowered back, doing no more than hiss at the invisible barrier Jace had made around him. Handy—he just wished he knew how the fuck he had done it. And if he would be able to do it again.

Popping a brow, he kept his hands out and stepped closer. The demons that made the writhing mass tried to reach him with snapping jaws, clicking claws, yet could not. They all screeched in a calliope of noise—disjointed and insane sounding. They hissed over and over, "Camden! Die! Camden! Die!" But they were unable to do more than make that shitload of noise.

Jace chanced another step and the mass mirrored in a retreating motion. Another and the same result. "Holy shit," he mumbled and then, let one hand drop, while the other dared to reach out to touch the mass. The moment his fingers touched, it a loud, excruciating sound ripped from the demons—dozens of voices merged into a single, hysterical one.

Jace let out an agonized yell, as pain sent him to his haunches. His arms wrapped around his head defensively from the excruciating decibel of the shrieking. The demon that had taken Amanda's form was writhing in pain and Jace actually had a moment of sympathy for it. He experienced the same agony. Fuck…he somehow screwed up majorly. In sync with the rest of his twisted education, Jace had no idea how or why.

Skylar wasn't sure if she heard a sound from where she sat on the bed in the other room. She had tried to send Kitt another text and hoped the woman had not caught the last flight for the day out of Cleveland. She heard another sound and this time, it caught more of her attention—a high pitched whining type of noise. "Did you guys hear that?"

Zane looked up from his phone, Alex her laptop, and Franklin sat up to listen for what she had heard. "No. Wait…" They were all on their feet now as Skylar approached the adjoining door to Jace's room. Opening it, she jerked her hand back when she found the knob ice cold. "Oh no." She grabbed it, even though the temperature was so frigid, her skin felt burnt, but she was able to throw open the door. Taken aback by what she witnessed, she was blocked from taking an instinctual flight or fight step back by the others behind her in the doorway.

Jace writhed on the bed and screamed out in his sleep. His voice raw and full of pain. Skylar glanced over her shoulder and saw no offering of advice coming from the rest of the crew. "What do we do? Usually Kitt handles this! I have no idea what to do." Jace let out another yell and the startling sound brought her focus back to him. "He needs to be woken up, right?"

Franklin stepped around her and approached the bed, his trepidation clear in both expression and movements. "I'll do it."

Skylar really didn't think that was a wise idea and she even reached out to stop him, her mouth open to protest, but it was too late. The moment the older man touched Jace, he reared up to grab Franklin by the throat and came off the bed faster than humanly possible. Franklin was forced to backstep until his back met the wall and Jace prowled in close with a snarl.

"Hey! Wait!" Skylar rushed forward to grab Jace's arms to pull him free. The man must be trapped in some freaky night terror that fueled the man's strength. Franklin's eyes were bugging out, his face going ruddy red. It was clear he was unable to breathe and his hands wrapped around Jace's wrist in a desperate attempt to break the hold. She screamed in his face, "Jace! Damn it! Wake up!"

"Jace!"

Skylar glanced sideways to see Kitt had returned and stood agape in the doorway as she took in the scene. The moment Kitt's voice cut through the chaos, Jace let Franklin go, sagged to the floor and hit it hard after he bounced off the side of the bed. Skylar shakily stepped back as Kitt ran forward to cradle Jace's head in her lap and combed her fingers through his hair. Franklin staggered away, having to catch himself on the dresser with one hand and the other clutched on his throat. He panted to restore his breathing to normal.

Kitt stayed on the floor with Jace and Skylar squatted on the floor in front of her. Kitt whispered with her head down and focused on Jace. "Not supposed to wake him up. You have to be careful." Her tone was softly gentle to comfort but it only set off Skylar's anger.

"Right. Well, we wouldn't know that since that's what *you* do." Skylar stood and glared down at her friend. She loved Kitt as any bestie should, but her behavior over the last week had been less than admirable. In fact, it bordered on a what-the-fuck level of bitchiness. Kitt lifted her head with shock on her face and Skylar ran out of steam and words. A snort of disbelief was all she could pull off before walking out of the room.

Zane followed to grasp her arm and she spun around to face him. "I need air, Zane. You can come with me or you can stay. Up to you." The man was wise enough to let her go and chose to follow. Getting outside, Skylar lit up a cigarette and lifted a finger as the man started to say something—most likely trying to convince her once again how dangerous the habit was. "Don't start. It's either I smoke this ciggy or I rip Kitt's hair out. You can decide which one I do on that front too, if you want."

Zane sighed and leaned on the rail in front of her on the narrow outside motel walkway. "You noticed she's way off too? Dude, I thought it was just me." His blue eyes went to the motel door. "I get it. This is all freaky, but to just leave like that? That's not like her at all." Zane brought his eyes back to Skylar's. "But maybe she's right. We are totally out of our league here, Sky. Not to say we were in one before, but this is night and day compared to that."

Skylar opened her mouth to rip Zane a new one for speaking his doubts, but she had not a single verbal platform to stand on. If the surfer boy was right, this was a completely different scenario than fighting the demons tormenting Jace and his late wife. Sure, they knew more now than they did then, but they were still trying to figure out what it all meant. "We were flying blind the first time. We are not so ignorant now, Zane."

Zane gave her a slight smile. "I think that might be the first time you didn't call me stupid, Sky."

She snorted once more and tossed the cigarette butt away. "I said we weren't so ignorant. Our collective smarts make up for your idiocy."

But she couldn't help but smile when she caught sight of Zane putting a hand on his chest. His expression composed of complete, if not amused, mock devastation as he responded, "That is so mean, Sky. But uh," he followed her back into the hotel room, "I'm still the good looking one, right?"

CHAPTER NINE

Amanda couldn't breathe and her struggles became useless—growing weaker and weaker by the second. One moment, they were traveling down the highway, Amanda once again trying to get Steven to understand her decision and him angry at her attempts. The next, the car went sharply to her right, off the road, and into the lake. The water that met them there was impossibly cold—there wasn't even ice on the road—it made zero sense in the split-second her mind used to consider.

Now upside down, pain shot through her body and the ear-splitting twisted sound of metal a horrifying symphony. She had instinctively braced with her hands on the dash and then they flew up involuntarily as they flipped. Now her head and shoulders were under water. It tasted horrible—vile and toxic, so her body naturally choked, which caused it to rush into her lungs. Within a minute, maybe two, she tried to suck oxygen through the fluid encapsulating her inside and outside to no avail.

Why wasn't Steven helping her? She tried to scream, as her arms thrashed and she tried to find the seat belt lock, only to find her hands weren't the only ones there. Turning her head in confusion, the hands were not those of her husband nor did they assist. They were doing the opposite. They were black and oily, yet weirdly hot within the cold temperature of the water. Her eyes tried to focus through the murk to see arms attached to a monster from hell. Her mind conjured up one word with its last dying synapse—a demon.

Amanda screamed.

Or that's what Jace thought, until he realized he not only screamed, but he was also the one that drowned.

Kitt's alarmed voice brought Jace around at the very same second the gagging did. Rolling to his side, he coughed and vomited vile, dark water as he choked to get it out of his chest. A painful process and when Kitt gave him room as she stumbled back, Jace moved to his hands and knees to gag the rest from his lungs onto the hotel room carpet.

"Baby, take it slow." Kitt returned quickly to rub his back and then to help climb to the bed. He wiped his mouth on his sleeve and panted to restore his panicked breathing to normal. He had been drowning.

Drowning he had experienced all through Amanda's body. Or memories. Or some fucked up way. The undeniable and baffling proof was in the dark, wet stained carpet next to the bed. "Demons. They wouldn't let her loose. In the car. They wanted her to drown." Jace used the headboard to stand, his legs unsteady and body feeling as if it was constructed from rubber. The others entered the room. "I saw things. From Amanda's point of view. It was either a nightmare or some other connection. Something…" His legs gave and he landed on his ass to sit on the bed. "But I know how to get to her. I just can't do it here."

Kitt let out what he feared was a relieved sigh. "Great. We can go home. I'll start packing."

Jace reached out to stop her and her blue eyes met his in confusion. He knew she hated being here, nor had he forgotten she had walked out. "No. I mean, I can't do it here. As in, awake. I have to go inside the nightmare realm to figure this out."

Kitt gasped and jerked her arm away. "No! Are you kidding me?"

Skylar stepped over to join them with Franklin right behind the women. "Jace, as pissed as I am with my best friend right now for doing such a bitch move earlier, I am going to have to agree with her. You came to soaking wet. Coughing up water. From a hotel bed. In Ohio. As far as I know, you don't even have a *view* of the crappy pool, much less took a swim in it before nap time."

Giving Skylar a "no shit" look, Jace swung his focus back on his girlfriend as he stood. The dizziness had begun to fade along with the weakness. Locking his eyes with Kitt's, he said to the others, "Can you guys leave us alone?" When no one moved, he transferred his gaze to meet each person's eyes. "Leave, now." He walked to the door and apparently, him being able to do that with a somewhat steady gait, they obeyed when he opened it. They all filed out, but Skylar paused to give him a concerned look before leaving. Closing the door behind them, he braced his hands on the wood and let out a slow exhale. "Kitt, you left. I really am trying to understand, but you're going to have to explain." He turned and let his back hit the door to lean against it. "Where did you go?"

Kitt chewed on her bottom lip and came over to wrap her arms around him. "I don't know why. I just got so angry. But that doesn't change the reason I'm worried." She lifted her head to rest her chin on his chest and brought her eyes up to his. "Something isn't right about all of this, baby. I don't know how to explain it." Her eyes then moved to the wet spot on the carpet. "You drowned. In your sleep. And it wasn't in your nightmare, but someone else's." Her eyes came back to his.

"*Someone* else's Jace. How are you going to have any control over that?"

Jace would have loved to have the perfect answer that would ease his girlfriend's mind, but the only one he could muster was a shrug, followed by a wince, which led into him looking at the floor. And knowing his Kitt like he did, that was not going to soothe her in the slightest. Exhaling slowly, he moved to sit on the end of the bed and took her hand in his as he lifted his chin to look up at her. "Kitt, I know you're worried. But I can't just leave with this unsolved. This woman needs me. And it's apparent that I am the only one that can help her."

"Or it's trap. The demons are once again setting one for you and you're going to walk right into it." Kitt said it so simply that it struck Jace how commonplace the bizarre had become in their lives over the past year. "And if you have to do it in the nightmare realm where none of us can help you, it's one that might work." She squatted down in front of him and his heart lurched at the desperation he found in her beautiful blue eyes. It also laced her tone as she whispered, "Please. If you love me, tell me we'll go home. Please."

"Baby, I can't do that, but you know I love you," Jace replied. She was being unusually desperate and Kitt had never been the type to piss and moan. But she had uncharacteristically done a large volume of both just in the past day alone. "Kitt, if there were any other choices or a chance she could get help from anyone else, believe me, I'd love to go home."

She jerked her hands from his grasp and gave him a look so scathing, Jace wondered if his wet clothes would steam from the angry heat of it. "Then a stranger means more to you than I do."

Jace was on his feet in disbelief. "That is bullshit and you know it." He paced away and then glared at her. "And let's not even discuss how you left and fucking were going to go home. Why did you even come back, Kitt? Care to explain that one?"

She took several steps away to reach the table, where her big messenger bag sat and for a moment, Jace thought she was going to do a repeat of her earlier exit. She stood there with her back to him and spine ramrod stiff. Jace crossed his arms as his anger-fueled confusion rode roughshod through the residual disorientation of the bizarre nightmare drowning.

However, his emotions flew around the room like a frantic sparrow a moment later, when she turned and held out an object in her hand. His eyes fixated on it even as his mind tried to reject the reality of what it meant. But as much as he would have liked to have an answer for the bafflement, his brain was no more help than it had been at suggesting a solution to Amanda's situation. He felt like he drowned in a different manner now.

His silence had Kitt nailing hopeful speculation into pure fact with two simple words. "I'm pregnant."

Jace's legs apparently forgot their purpose as they folded and his ass hit the foot of the bed to sit. Reaching out, he took the pregnancy test and there was zero doubt with the word 'pregnant' and its smiley icon shown as if to celebrate. How the fuck a stick could begin to presume that happiness would always follow in every single positive result, he had no idea. He even shook it like it was an Etch-a-Sketch and it, in turn, would change from the motion. But no, it still stated the same detail. *Pregnant. Be happy about it, asshole. The smiley face says so.*

"You're pregnant." His voice sounded wooden and strange as he lifted his eyes to hers. "With my baby."

And just like that, Jace's whole world spun and part of him wanted to get off. This was a ride he was ill-suited to be on and not one he ever thought he'd get a ticket to.

"Are you kidding me? You're pregnant!"

Jace should have known that Skylar wouldn't have left them alone for long and he was proven right when she burst in, ready to interfere, and overheard the pregnancy declaration. Her earlier disgruntlement at her best friend clearly forgiven, she pulled Kitt into a hug and cheered the news.

He, on the other hand, sat there staring at the pregnancy stick as if it would be more forthcoming with more information. Of course, he had not worn a condom every time he and Kitt had made love, but enough to lower the odds of a baby. Not to mention, he had tried for so long with Laura and yet, they were never able to conceive. Sure, he had never had it validated by a medical professional, but he ignorantly presumed his sterility. Given the myriad of drugs, cocktails of concoctions given to him since childhood to either control a psychosis by doctors or exorcise some demon by his mother, it wasn't without believable reason. He and his late wife had wanted a baby so bad. Both wondered and desperately hoped, as many troubled couple did, that if they brought a child into the mix, it would repair the tattered fabric of their marriage. It had been the basis of several arguments that resulted in Laura's wails of her uselessness and Jace's belief in his worthlessness.

He wanted to tell Skylar to leave, but before he had a chance, Alex, Franklin, and Zane were filing in and had been told the news. Kitt had remained silent, even as Skylar bubbled with excitement, hugging her. Lifting his eyes to Kitt's, his mouth opened, yet no words came from its depths. How could he describe the overwhelming joy battling with the equally conquering, spine-freezing fear he felt at the concept of a baby? His baby. Not just with her, but with anyone.

Franklin had come over, but Jace didn't acknowledge his appearance until the man clapped a hand on his shoulder. "Congrats, Jace. This is wonderful."

Jace's brow creased as he regarded him. "Is it?" He swung his head down to view the evidence and nodded, even as the shock squeezed a mental vice grip on his grey matter. "It is. Yeah. We're going to have a baby."

But the words felt flat and as Franklin pulled him up into a hug, Jace eyes swung back to meet Kitt's again. He found disappointment and even worse, fear in those blue depths.

He had to wonder…did she see the same in his?

CHAPTER TEN

"You don't want the baby?"

Jace excused himself from the crew's celebration, went to the bar, ordered a strong whiskey on ice, and now sat next to the pool at the motel. There were no guests and the pool itself was covered with a tarp for the upcoming off-season—the air already chill with encroaching winter.

Glancing back to see Skylar, he faced back forward as he bit an ice cube in half with his teeth. "It's not that. Not even close. How could I not want a baby? With the woman I love?" She moved around to sit in a chair in front of him and he met her eyes. "But how am I supposed to deal with that and everything else? I lose sleep now worrying about Kitt. Keeping her safe. To pray that demons don't try to use her to get to me." He rose to his feet and took the last ice cube into his mouth. "*Again*. But now, I have a baby inside of her womb for them to get? A tiny, helpless human inside of Kitt. I can't put an amulet on that baby, can I? What do I do? Make her never sleep again? Or when she does, I stay wide awake and pray I somehow know, with soul warrior skills I don't even understand, much less," he let out a bitter laugh, "know how to use, will say 'hey, idiot, demon buffet on your baby's soul.'" He threw the glass into the pool, it clipped the concrete edge and shattered as it sliced through the tarp to splash below. "Smiley fucking face."

"Wow, feel better now, idiot?"

Jace turned to find Skylar looking almost amused at his outburst and it was not unsurprising. She was his best friend for a reason. Exhaling out a long breath, he dropped back down to sit as he brought his hands up to rub over his face. "Not really, no." Looking away, he closed his eyes and hunched his shoulders up. "And you're right. I was an idiot and a complete asshole in how I handled it. Shit, but Sky…" his hands dropped as his eyes opened to meet hers, "A baby. They will, hell, if they hadn't already, seek that baby out and use it to get to me. We both know that. If not destroy my baby before he or she ever has a chance to be born alive. And a year ago? Two? I would have found that fantastical to consider. Now? Knowing how far they would go to take hits at my happiness, we both know it's a very real possibility."

Sky reached out to place a hand on his knee. "I get all of that, buddy. I swear I do. But what can you do? Sure, you and Kitt have options as far as the pregnancy. But I also know the both of you. This was unplanned. Not predicted, but if anyone has been conditioned for that shit, it's you and Kitt. You know a baby would be amazing. You love her. She loves you. A baby is just a given sometimes with a love that strong. And think about it." She moved to squat on her haunches in front of him. "That baby was conceived in the darkest time of your relationship. Yet, life started in the nightmare that your life had been then. An innocent, amazing gift for surviving it. That alone means you need to focus on the good and find joy in this. That baby is yours. It's a fighter from the moment of conception. It's a Camden."

She gave him a smile and wiped a tear glistening on her lashes. "And with Kitt as a mother, no demons could stand a chance of hurting that baby. And you have the Dead Man's Crew--still needing t-shirts by the way--to help. It's going to be okay, Jace." She moved forward to encircle him in a tight hug. "I know it. Now, stop being an asshole and go in there and tell the mother of your baby it's going to be okay. Even if you don't fully believe it, you need to make sure she does." She pulled back to cup his face in her hands. "Fake it until you make it, idiot."

By the time Jace made his way back to the hotel room, the others had left to leave him and Kitt alone. She sat in one of the chairs by the hotel window, chin in her hand and eyes looking out beyond to the parking lot. Letting out a slow sigh, he walked over and knelt on the floor in front of her. Without speaking a word, he laid his head in her lap and closed his eyes when her fingers started combing through his hair.

They stayed that way for several minutes and it was Jace who found the bravery to broach the subject that hung expectantly between them. "We're having a baby." Yes, he had said those words before, but this time, rather than the flat emotion behind them, joy dared to be brave too, as it crept into his tone. He looked up at her and his voice cracked in amazed awe. "We're going to have a baby, Kitt."

She had tears in those beautiful blue eyes, as she nodded. She gave no reply, but she brought her head down to meet his and the kiss that followed spoke all he needed to know. Standing, he brought her upward with him without breaking their physical connection. Walking backwards with her until they reached the bed, he broke that link long enough for him to tug her shirt off and Kitt did the same with his. Kissing down her neck as her hands slid over his back, he no longer flinched when his lover's touch grazed the dozens of scars. He no longer tried to hide his nudity from her scrutiny when they became undressed. When her fingers tips teased down his thighs, where more puckered scars could be found, it did nothing more than inflame his desire, rather than quell it.

Staying above her on his forearms, the sheet pulled over them both, he focused on her passion-flushed face below him. "I love you. And I love our baby. And it's going to be fine. I will make sure of it." His fingers moved up to brush hair from her face before he lowered his head to kiss her once again. She tasted salty from the tears so recently shed, but he was determined he would do all he could to prevent any from fears from happening again.

As they teased each other, words replaced with moans, he went to enter her and she put a hand on his chest to stop him. Gasping, he halted and looked down at her in heated confusion. "Kitt, what's wrong?"

Her eyes fluttered open and she gasped with a smile, "Guess I don't need to say we need a condom, huh?" A small lusty giggle followed. "Sorry. Habit."

Jace couldn't help but laugh, even if it was ragged and hoarse with passion. "No, I think we're good for the next nine months, baby." He smiled and dipped down to kiss her again. "We'll use the condom money to stock up on ice cream and pickles."

CHAPTER ELEVEN

Jace and Kitt made love with the untethered passion stirred by life and death stress—perhaps the only positive about all this. Holding her close, he had then fallen into a deep sleep where dreams or nightmares always waited no matter how much he prayed they would choose elsewhere to be. But as his eyes opened, he realized he was not in either one.

He was in a memory.

At first he was confused. He knew he slept but he also knew this was from the past. Lifting his head, he saw the homemade straps his mother had created to tie Jace down to the bed. She had stopped that practice when he was nine. Jace learned how to escape them. In his sleep.

She would find him in his bedroom closet the next day. She would scream at him and demand to know how he did it but he had no idea. All he knew was he woke up in the closet. She would then go ballistic and rant that the demons did it so he could kill her in his sleep. A lock was then secured to his bedroom door to the outside. And she would lock it with the key worn on a ribbon around her neck. Jace's recall of this particular night began to emerge from the fog of sleep as he watched it all unfold as it had then through the eyes of him as a seven-year old.

Turning his head, Jace could make out the dozens of crucifixes nailed to the walls. The painted by his mother crosses and the word Jesus. Over and over. The rest of the available space were printouts, posters, even pamphlets from churches listing the glory of God and promises of salvation. Other children had movie posters and magazine clippings of their favorite celebrity. But not young Jace Camden. He had his insane mother's attempts to keep the demons she believed her son harnessed contained within this small bedroom.

There were voices in the hall. His mother's and that of a man he did not recognize.

"I don't want you here! I told you not to come here!" His mother's tone shrill and angry.

"I want to see my son. I need to make sure you haven't done it yet." The man's voice was deep but held a tremor. Was the man desperate? And Mommy done what yet?

"You know I should have. But I can't. I need to. But I can't. If I do it, the demons get out of the holes." There was a thud on the wall. The sound Jace thought was a body hitting it, like when Mommy shoved him back into his room when he tried to sneak into the kitchen for something to eat. She sometimes forgot to feed him. But even those attempts were when the hunger made his stomach hurt really bad.

"You are insane," the man said the word and the Jace could detect anger. The doorknob rattled and his mother screamed. Jace jerked in his restraints—was the man a good man? Or a bad man? Jerking on the binds, he felt the cords cut into his skin but he was used to that and he already had scars from when Mommy forgot they were on and she left him tied there for days. Or when she tied them too tight even when he cried and told her they were.

"I'm insane!? Me? You dare to call me that after what you saw? You saw and you ran. Who stayed to take care of *my* son? Because he was no longer yours when you walked out that door." His mother then laughed, the type of laugh that scared Jace. He even, embarrassed to think of, peed the bed a few times when Mommy did it in the corner of his room. She would rock and talk a strange language. Then she would laugh, that very same laugh.

"Just let me take him. Then you don't have to be worried about the demons getting to you. I'll take the boy and you won't have to fight it anymore." The man's voice changed yet again—this time concerned and sad. That confused Jace. Why would a strange man care about him? It was clear he knew about the demons Mommy said he brought into their lives. Wasn't the man scared? And why was he sad?

Jace opened his mouth to cry out to the both of them. He wanted to see the man. Who was he, why did he care? But then there was a slap and another thud against his door. Jace knew that sound—Mommy would slap him too if he made a sound. Just like he was told to be silent when the people in the city cars came by. When Mommy lied and said he was at school. Or at a friend's house. Jace knew they were lies because he missed school all the time to hide the marks. Healing cuts of crosses Mommy said would let the demons see the knife—so they would not come out where she could kill them. The ones inside of Jace.

"No. You can't take him. I have to do what needs to be done. And I'm the only one that can…"

Jace sat up with a yell and gulped air into his lungs.

"Baby?"

Swallowing, he looked over at Kitt who had a look of concern, easy to see even in the darkness of the hotel room. "Bad dream? Are you here? Jace?"

He nodded to let her know he was fully aware and awake before he dropped down to lay on the bed. Bringing a hand up to fold over his eyes, he commanded himself to breathe in slowly and exhale even slower. "There was a man. When I was a kid. Someone trying to stop my mom from doing…" He didn't often talk about his childhood and when he did, it was the barest of details. Turning his head to make out Kitt's face as it hovered over him with worry, he brought a hand up to press his palm against her cheek. "You're going to be an amazing mother to our child. You know that, right?"

Kitt smiled. Jace felt the rise of her dimple and cheek as her face formed the smile. "You think, I don't know. My mom is pretty great. Dad too. But me, I am the queen of screwing up and never finishing what I start."

Jace chuckled as his other hand found her belly at his side; his fingers splaying over it. "Kind of impossible to stop what we've started now." His eyes sought hers. "And that makes me so fucking happy. I want this baby. I want to have you be the mother of my baby. And I want to be the father that I never had."

He felt warm, wet tears against his fingers. These were the good kind. Jace knew his woman well enough to know that. She brought her head down and her warm lips pressed over his to seal in an unspoken promise. One that need not be said for Kitt Thomas understood Jace Camden's heart like no other had cared to learn.

Jace would do anything for this child to have the childhood he was never given a chance to have. Go to Hell and back to protect Kitt and their baby. The words had no need for Jace to voice—because Kitt believed in him. In every way.

CHAPTER TWELVE

The next morning, Jace had requested everyone join him and Kitt in their hotel room. Alex had brought them all coffee, Franklin some weird tasting bran muffins, and Kitt had taken two bites before she ran to the bathroom to puke up that small amount of food. As everyone pretended not to hear her puking in the close quarters, Zane failed and that was when they all learned he was a sympathy puker. Once they endured a second session of Zane throwing up, who somehow chased it with more coffee and muffins, they got to down to the subject at hand.

"I can't help Amanda from home. We have to do it here." He and Kitt had stayed up half of the night discussing what he felt he needed to do. She was still afraid and he was as well, but now they were a united front to figure out how to help Amanda and do so quickly, in order to go home and enjoy the pregnancy. Added to that, Jace would be hyper-protective until they returned and Kitt did not want him carrying that high-level of stress and the impact it would have on his weakened heart condition.

Glancing over at her and getting a nervous, but encouraging smile, Jace continued. "We have to get me alone with her. Without that asshole husband of hers in the way. I need to find her in the nightmare realm, where the demons are holding her soul. Find out why and how. Then, just like before, I need to put myself in the moment they got their claws in her. And for that, we need a car. Some water. And it has to be fucking cold."

The plan was made. The timeline figured out. Franklin had started to help secure the supplies and Alex was going to try to use her influence at the facility to allow Jace time alone with Amanda. And Zane and Skylar? They were tasked with getting a rental car, which had them standing in one of the dozens of the rental agencies in Cleveland. Holding Jace's credit card, used for the online reservation, Skylar was fidgeting by biting on her nail as the clerk assisted the customer in front of them.

Zane, on the other hand… was driving her insane.

"Stop," she said under her breath as the man was making a series of popping noises with his tongue against his cheek. She slid her eyes sideways to see him and then narrowed when he smiled. And let out another pop. "Seriously, I'm going to find a way to make you be a passenger in this rental car when Jace does this crazy plan of his."

Zane gasped and Skylar took some smug joy in the very real threat she had just made and the consequences of it. Especially when the clerk called them to the counter with a well-practiced, if not fake smile.

"Oh, you got the full-coverage insurance. It covers everything. It is an upgrade on the price. We do offer a lower-cost insurance you can use in combination with any liability. Would you like to hear about that package?"

Zane started laughing and Skylar stabbed him in the side with a well-manicured nail before addressing the clerk. "No. We want as much coverage as we can get on the car." She, too, was smiling. The one she used when it involved the law firm where she once worked at as a paralegal, when representing a client they were pretty sure was as guilty as a criminal could be. "In fact, in regard to that insurance…it covers collision, damage," she hoped the shrug enhanced the question and came off as nonchalant, "driving it into a lake, right?"

The clerk's plastic-like smile did not even waver and Skylar had to give her credit for that. But her tell was a slow blinking, as she processed the question. "Excuse me? May I ask what you plan on using the rental for?"

Skylar noticed the clerk slowly slid the key fob back towards herself and away from them. Shit…

"Nah, oh, come on. That's just silly." Zane moved to rest his arms on the counter and gave the clerk an eyeful of toned, tan forearms. He put on his best smile and wore it easily from his time as a former surfer doing publicity for the sport. The fact he was good looking with a sun kissed tan, he stood out among the pale skinned Ohioans. Sky was sure a clerk, living on the Great Lakes, had never met a guy like Zane— good looking, sweet, and flirty without even trying. Skylar had to stop her jaw from dropping, as the clerk bought the act one hundred percent as her suspicious manner deteriorated in the easy-going force of Zane's flirting. Skylar was baffled at Zane's romantic skills were confirmed when the clerk let out a schoolgirl-like giggle.

"I just have to ask, you know?" The clerk moved to put an elbow on the counter, resting her chin on it, bringing her closer to Zane with a dreamy smile. "I'm sure it's nothing. But it's full-coverage, so it would cover everything." Her voice went a little husky. "Anything you need. I can help you with all kinds of things, too."

Skylar rolled her eyes at the exchange but did notice that Zane used his fingers to take the key fob, no longer retreating, into his hand. Well, damn, she had a new respect for the guy. Not that she would ever admit it to him. Or anyone. Ever.

Restoring her friendly façade, as Zane pulled back with keys secured, Skylar gave the clerk a smile as she handed over the credit card, along with her driver's license. The clerk bounced away and put far too much effort to sway her ass seductively as she did. Skylar elbowed Zane's side and said low, "Smooth. I didn't know you had it in you."

Zane's smile became smug as he returned a sideways glance. "There's all kinds of things in me you may not have noticed, Sky." He then turned his head and bent in to whisper, "Let me know if you want to see other skills you may not be aware of." Zane winked. "Yet."

Skylar's jaw failed not to drop as he then turned away to go check out the car's gas levels as well as scratches and dents with the clerk. Like that was *even* going to matter if this plan proceeded as discussed. And she would be damned if this time, it was her checking out a certain ass as it walked away—and not the cute clerk's butt. When Skylar realized she paused to consider Zane's ass or any part of the man, she shook her head as she followed, mumbling, "No. No. No, you do not want to ponder that idiot's other skills."

But it was too late. Skylar's mind had already gone there.

"It's just a simple meeting. I would like to point out that it was you that requested our help. And when I suggested that Jace could be of help, it was you who asked me to include him. Now, after one meeting, you won't let him try to assist Mrs. Bishop?"

Alexis' nerves were frazzled. Actually, they were in that state when she had arrived at the posh mental facility. Now, they were barely hanging on as she sat in Doctor Lewis' office. She had been informed, rather abruptly, again upon arrival that she and her associates were no longer allowed at the facility. She hoped to appeal to Dr. Lewis' better nature, but apparently, he didn't have one. That or Steven Bishop had browbeaten the doctor into compliance or made promises; Alex had no idea.

"Alexis, I cannot override what the patient's husband has demanded. While I will admit, what happened previously was bizarre, it still doesn't change policy and procedures." He sat back, removed his glasses, and rubbed his eyes with his fingertips. "She's less responsive and he's met with a private hospice group to bring her home." His hand dropped and he met Alexis' gaze with one filled with exhaustion. "We both know what that means. He's given up and he just wants this to end. But let's be honest," Dr. Lewis sat forward and tented his fingers in front of him on the desk, "Amanda is no longer technically here. Just a human shell."

Alexis was on her feet, her palms coming down on the desk in front of him, and lowered herself to glare, eye-to-eye. "You've also given up on her. Something we should never do with our patients, no matter how frustrating it would be!" Yes, Alexis had given up on Jace once and still felt guilty about it, but it had been a hard-won lesson. One that she knew others in her field would never be forced to be educated on. The supernatural was an aspect never instructed in the books with any solid information; rather, it was viewed as ludicrous and comical. Yes, she had been that way as well, once-upon-a-time, until she met the very real demons that tormented Jace Camden. What an eye-opening learning curve it had been for Alexis—but not surprising when others in her field did not even entertain supernatural causes.

"Dr. Martinez, I know you are frustrated, coming all this way from Texas, only to be unable to assist or solve the issues for Mrs.

Bishop. But I cannot grant your request or Mr. Camden's to see my patient." He sighed and met her eyes. "Or more precisely, my former patient. As I have said, her husband has made other arrangements." He then put his hand over Alex's on the desk and she was about to jerk it away from his touch in disgust, until she realized what the man had done.

Glancing down without saying a word, she found the small thumb drive he had placed between two of her fingers. Alexis gave him a confused look as Dr. Lewis widened his eyes, as if the gesture would explain the silence what he could not do with words. The man had not given up on Amanda—he was just not sure what else *he* could do.

Standing upright stiffly, Alex wrapped her hand around the drive as she picked up her purse. One hand came up to shove her glasses back up her nose, as she mouthed, "thank you" before leaving Dr. Lewis' office.

The whole Dead Man's Crew minus Alex had gathered in the hotel room Franklin was sharing with Zane, eating two delivered pizzas and soda from the machine down the hall. Kitt was picking at the toppings, as she tried to eat, but her morning sickness, saddled with nerves, wreaked havoc on her appetite. Jace had been spoiling her rotten and most likely, it would be *him* she would be sick of within weeks, if not days. The meal had been enjoyable with light banter and a touch of excitement about the pregnancy, but that was halted when Alex arrived to let them know Jace had been denied another meeting with Amanda.

"It's pointless, if I can't see her," Jace said at the news.

"He did give me this," Alex said as she held up a flash drive before tossing it on the table with a frustration that they all felt. "I believe it's footage of her sessions."

Jace gave it a glimpse and then looked away. "Great. Video of their sessions won't give me squat. I need to be in the room with her again. I already know I can get to where she is. I just need to let her demons know, so they'll show themselves. It's key for me to determine how strong their hold on her is." He stood, picking up the drive to toss in his duffel bag, before pacing. "Fuck," he grumbled as he raked his fingers through his hair.

"Does that mean we can go home?"

Kitt's question stopped Jace in his tracks, in order to formulate an answer—he honestly had no idea. Did it? Sure, he had a plan on how to put himself within the nightmare trapping Amanda, but he needed a connection by touch with the woman to enable him to see any masked demon attached to her soul. But now? He just didn't know—just like most everything with his new "role" in the realm of death, life, and demons. He made his way to the hotel window and rubbed his forehead as he looked down at the pool. The cuts from the broken glass still appeared in the dark cloth, giving him a glimpse of the cold water beneath, when the winter sunlight hit it just right.

"We will still try to get to her." He heard the murmurs of questions behind him and could have made a high-dollar bet on the shock and disappointment on Kitt's face. Turning gave him proof he would have won. "We will see if these mythical, magical powers I don't know shit about can at least give me a way to reach Amanda." He met Kitt's eyes and exhaled slowly. "And then, we go home. Our flight leaves on Friday. That doesn't change. Which gives us tomorrow to carry out the plan. Then," his voice softened, as he moved back to squat down in front of Kitt and place his hand over her stomach, "we all go home."

CHAPTER THIRTEEN

Skylar had needed a drink. Which led to a second one and then a third. One would think since they had killed her best friend, Jace, once before that the second attempt at doing so would be easier. Less taxing on the nerves. And to think such would be stupid. She hated it the last time and hated the thought of having to do it again even more. Skylar prided herself on learning from her mistakes and never having to repeat any error in judgement. She was ethical and intelligent, moral, and loaded to the brim with common sense. But here they were, once again, strategizing on how to get away with murder—literally—murder. And though they had been able to bring Jace back the second time… wait, that was not correct. *They* had not brought the man back—the spirit, ghost, energy, whatever the fuck esoteric term used for Jace's late wife pulling the Lazarus trick, was the one responsible.

"Another," Skylar said as she leaned over the hotel bar to get the bartender's attention.

"She's had enough."

The bartender nodded as if *she* was not the one paying her tab. Squeezing her eyes shut, they opened when she turned on the bar stool to find Zane standing there. "Excuse me? Last time I checked, I was over the drinking age of twenty-one and you were not my fucking daddy. Nor husband. Nor, well, anything really." She gave him her snarkiest smile as she slapped her palm on the bar. "In fact, you are a speck of annoyance in my day-to-day existence." She emphasized with a small space between her finger and thumb before she turned her back to him. "Hey! You!" She yelled at the bartender. "I said another drink!"

Suddenly, Skylar was jerked off the stool, stumbling on her heels, and moved towards the hotel lobby as Zane held her arm to steer the movement. "Stop it!" She jerked out of his grasp and shoved him back. "Seriously! I've had three drinks, Zane, and they were watered down. Which is a shame," the volume of her voice rose in order for both the hotel staff and guests to have no choice but to overhear, "at the prices this place charges!"

"Stop it." Zane had reached the elevators with her in tow, but Skylar was so pissed, she moved to slap him. But rather than being able to give his stupid, tanned face a resounding smack, her wrist was caught in Zane's free hand.

"I'm scared too. Do you hear me? I'm scared too, Sky."

His words quelled her fire to fight as she met Zane's blue eyes. How had she not noticed how blue they were before? Perhaps it was because they were seated within his boyishly handsome, tanned face. Or maybe it was the soft, sun-bleached, long hair that perfectly framed his features without the man doing a damn thing with it. But besides noticing the hue of his gaze, Skylar found fear within their depths she recognized. Felt a kinship to.

Afterall, they had both been friends with Jace for the same amount of time. Almost from the first week Jace had arrived in Galveston, they had befriended the lost and apparently, haunted man. Before that? She and Zane hadn't even known the other existed; they ran in totally different social circles. Completely different lifestyles. Skylar, a cut-throat, high-level law firm paralegal with tunnel vision on enhancing her career. Zane with no real ambition to get ahead, as he happily ran his grandfather's surf shop. All this demon, "life-and-death" shit forced Skylar to adapt beyond her borderline obsessive nature and boxed-in structured control. Adapting had created cracks in Skylar's orderly walls and had caused Zane's easy manner to take up residence. She had not even noticed the intrusion and now was not sure if it was welcomed or not. She would have to thank Jace for that…if the asshole survived tomorrow.

Jace had brought them together. He was the common integer in the circle of strangers that made up what they all amusingly called The Dead Man's Crew. Because of Jace, a group of strangers now formed a crew of friends. Together, they learned to believe in the unseen. That the impossible—even if it meant toying with death—could be possible.

"I thought you said all this was cool." Skylar's voice cracked as they stood there together waiting on the elevator. "You didn't even raise a concern when we discussed this earlier. You just sat there, nodding with that stupid smile on your face." She pulled her hand free, but replaced it on his chest with a smack, followed by her forehead moving forward to rest over it. "All you could talk about was that ridiculous Go-Pro camera set-up."

"It's all a cover, Sky. Total bullshit. I thought you were the smart one?"

Skylar snorted without lifting her head. "Right, whatever." But something about his tone had her lifting her eyes to meet his. "Why? He needs to hear the truth. The doubts."

Zane exhaled slowly, his back hitting the wall between the two elevators. "Why? He hears enough of that from you. The others. Do you think my adding to the negativity is going to change his mind? Is going to make any of this easier for him? Maybe, he needs for just one person to make it a little easier on him, Sky. He's the dude about to die. Not me. If I can make him smile a few times before he does, it has value."

He pushed off and came right up against her, his eyes flared with intensity as they bore into hers. "I *have* value. Beyond being the comic relief you and the rest seem to think I am. You just now took the time to see it." He gave her a slight smile. "And that's okay too. I'm used to that."

Zane was right. Skylar had discounted him as nothing more than a goofy guy she had to tolerate because Jace called him a friend. But as he spoke, his face showed an expression of hurt. It fled right before he smiled, but it was enough to expand Skylar's view of the man.

"Wait…" But the elevator arrived and Zane stepped inside it to go back to his room. Skylar wasn't sure if it was the liquor or the gravity of the task ahead of them. Maybe it was as simple as viewing Zane clearly for the first time, but she followed, stepped in, and kissed him.

His lips were incredibly warm and soft. As was the hand that came up to wrap against the nape of Skylar's neck. When he sighed into her mouth as his tongue greeted hers, it was sweet like the jellybeans he liked to eat—licorice…erotic yet light and fun. Just like the man himself.

The elevator reached their floor and Zane frowned as their lips moved apart. He appeared just as confused as Skylar at where the night was headed. Not that it mattered. She had already made up her mind.

If not allowed to get drunk in order to forget about everything, he would be her distraction. Maybe, just maybe, Zane needed the same. Taking his hand, she led him to the room she shared with Alex. She knew the doctor was in Franklin's room to tighten up their plans for tomorrow—she heard the woman's voice as they passed that door.

"Sky, what are we doing?" Zane asked a very sensible question. Funny how they had switched roles. Zane leaning to logic and Sky jumping into spontaneity as they entered the room.

She had the door half-closed and paused to hang the 'Do Not Disturb' sign on the outside knob before she closed it and engaged the swing lock. Still facing it, she slowly turned around and shrugged. "Were you planning on sleeping? I wasn't. Want to help me stay awake?"

She walked up to him to run her hands under his shirt and found hardened abs. Why had she never considered his physical build until recently? Another detail never given thought when it came to Zane. "Just shut up and be my distraction."

Zane dipped his head down with a smug smile and claimed her mouth. That meshing of their lips fired a passion their earlier one had been too timid to spark. It was commanding, as were his hands that ran down her back before cupping her ass. With little effort, he picked her up and carried her to the bed. Standing her up on it, he tugged off his shirt and then ran his hands under hers to cup her breasts in the expensive bra. Soon, he'd learn she wore silk panties that matched. Skylar did love her nice things with or without a lover to appreciate them. "Oh shit," Skylar thought, this would make Zane Miller her lover.

When Zane unbuttoned her shirt and tossed it, his heated gaze tracked upward, full of desire and arousal. His fingers were steadfast. His hands knew exactly where to be placed. There was no laughing goofball in the man in front of her now. Zane had transformed into a sure and confident lover or maybe, like the rest, she had never bothered to consider he always had been. Skylar would rather take credit for something in this flipped version of a relationship. The bra was left on and he gently, almost lovingly, helped her step out of her slacks, which hit the floor.

Her OCD wanted to scream for him to pick the items up, fold them, and place them in the chair. The aroused, wild Skylar said "fuck it." Because that's what she wanted to do now more than any other instinct…

Fuck Zane. And this time, Skylar meant it literally.

He pushed her back on the bed and she fell to lay on the scratchy, cheap hotel bedspread. Watching him undress, Skylar bit her bottom lip as she unabashedly watched the process. Long, lean body with zero tan lines—just golden, blonde-hair dusted skin and muscles that rippled with each move, subtle or grand. When he joined her on the bed, capturing her mouth with his to kiss, she made it very clear what she wanted and needed as she explored his body with bold touches and wanton moans.

But Zane had plans of his own, as his mouth moved away and then so did he. Skylar let out a frustrated sound as she moved to sit, but his hand reached up to press between her breasts to push her back down on the bed. "What are you doing? Zane? Foreplay? Really?"

Zane chuckled and even that sound was a turn-on to Sky. "Yes, really. You can't really ride a wave until you learn how it flows, Sky. Let me surf." He then trailed a series of flesh-tingling kisses and nips down her stomach and settled between her thighs. He looked up with a wicked smile before he dipped his head down and Skylar's fell back on the bed with a deep groan of pleasure.

Skylar would never call him "surfer boy" again. Doing so would bring memories of the waves he caused in that bed to the surface, flowing through the cracks—like Zane into her life. She cried out with her fingers fisted in his hair as another climax crested and he rode the surf of her pleasure with a growl.

Surfing became Skylar's favorite sport.

CHAPTER FOURTEEN

Jace's nerves were a frazzled mess, but not surprising, considering. They were about to drown him to the point of hyperthermia, seconds before death. They ran through their plans once again as they sat, gathered around a table in his hotel room. The standard continental breakfast had been left untouched on a paper plate in front of Jace. Coffee, of course, had not only been drunk, but refilled twice. He might even go for a third and why not? Did it stand a chance of keeping him awake? Hah, highly unlikely.

"So, we set up the car to go into the lake. Is it even cold enough to make me get to hypothermia?" His eyes went to the sliver of the lake he could see from the room's window. "Okay. It goes down the boat ramp, into the water, and I drown. Just like Amanda did." He got to his feet, paper coffee cup slowly rotating in his fingertips as he moved. "That, *hopefully*, will have me on the other side, where she's trapped. To see how she's being held there. And then, it's a matter of knowing the demons and hunting the demons." He stopped to look at the others. "Sounds easy enough."

Franklin was sipping some odd-smelling tea he claimed eased nerves. He did not appear at ease in the slightest. "We're going to pack you in ice, as well. I believe that, combined with the sudden cold snap the region is under, will suffice to get your temperature to that point. Alex and I are prepared with warming blankets and heated IV fluids.

CPR, of course, if needed." Franklin gave Kitt an understanding smile. "But I don't believe we'll need that measure."

Kitt's hand tightened on Jace's thigh and he kissed the side of her head, when she laid it on his shoulder. "Okay, all that sounds fucking amazing," he said, with more than enough snark to make it clear it was anything but. "What about witnesses? Someone stopping us?"

Zane laid out a print-out of a Google map. "I spent time watching the traffic and they have public cameras. There isn't one on this last boat ramp. And the flow of people coming and going is minimal, due to a construction detour. They are doing repairs one street over, so most through traffic is diverted. It's ideal. As far as cops? I can't find a schedule of routine checks. I think it's as clear of interference as we can get, driving you into a lake to die." He cracked a smile, but then Skylar glared at him and he cleared his throat. "Sorry."

Jace was about to transition to his part in the plan, when he noticed the interaction between his two friends was different. Well, beyond the fact they were about to assist in another dead-again scenario. Maybe it was the way Zane angled his head to give Skylar a look Jace had not witnessed before. Perhaps, in the way her glare went from reprimanding to… melting? It fit how Skylar not only backed off fast, but the approving smile from Zane when she had. "What's going on with you two?"

Both Skylar's and Zane's heads snapped to look at Jace, both jaws opened and sputtering sounds, rather than words. This, of course, only solidified Jace's belief that something strange was afoot with his two friends.

Kitt had sat forward and pointed a finger at the two of them. "You know, you two *are* acting really weird." She glanced over at Alex and Franklin, who joined in to analyze Zane and Sky as well.

Skylar attempted to give her trademarked look of disinterest. Zane tried to disarm the scrutiny by looking around, up, to the left, and then the right. It was so comedic that Jace expected the man to just yell out "squirrel" to try to redirect everyone's attention. But unlike Skylar, who could keep up a topic filibuster for hours, Zane had no such resilience.

"Fine! We had sex!" He caved within seconds, as he waved a hand frantically from him to Skylar, as if to make sure his sexual partnership was clearly defined to her, rather than Franklin who sat on his opposite side. "Skylar and me. Last night. For hours. We did it in so many posit…" He then let out a loud yelp and a thud rattled the table, as someone's knee struck the underside of the table. Jace could assume Zane had been struck by Skylar's heel coming down on his foot. Jace had been on the receiving end of that move more than once. A physically painful method of her saying, "shut up" and "you are an idiot," without saying a word.

Everyone stared at the two of them as Skylar smacked Zane and he tried to defend himself. The tussle quickly increased in intensity to such a level that Franklin was knocked off the end of the booth to land ungraciously on the floor with a grunt.

"We said we weren't going to tell anyone! We said we'd wait until we killed him first!" Skylar's tone was both reprimanding and embarrassed as she hit Zane. He yelped, as he tried to escape her wrath.

That, of course, coincided with the moment the waitress came to refill their coffee. The empty glass pot hit the floor. Dropped, due to shock at the woman hearing Skylar's last remark. Alex launched to her feet to explain it as a running joke. Kitt covered her mouth, eyes wide in amusement at the situation and Franklin scurried on his hands and knees to find his eyeglasses.

Jace started laughing. How could he not? A loud, full laugh that had the whole Crew freezing in place to look at him. "You two?" His finger pointing from Zane to Skylar. "Had sex?" His laughter deepened and he placed his hands on his stomach. His forehead went to the table to rest next to his plate of eggs. "Oh god, why does that make all of this somewhat worth it?"

Kitt's demeanor switched to one of concern. She rubbed his back and asked him if he was okay. Skylar had ceased her attack on Zane and now, the both were concerned for him as well. Alex still stood next to the waitress, each woman wearing expressions of bafflement for completely different reasons.

"Now look what you did! You broke him!" Skylar declared in a yell and resumed to beating Zane, who squeaked, as he finally made it out of the booth, only to head-butt Franklin as the man stood with glasses in hand.

Jace laughed harder and it wasn't until Kitt cupped his face in her hands, her face awash with worry, that he was able to dial it back a little. "Baby, are you okay?"

He nodded and brought a hand up to wipe tears of mirth from his eyes. "I'm fine. Seriously, this is the most fun I've had in months." He brought a hand up to graze his knuckles along her cheek and regarded the rest of the Crew. "But come on. You two hooking up? I can't begin to label that type of relationship. But can we not discuss the TMI details on the same day I'm about to die?" He smiled and forced himself to contain more laughter at their shocked expressions. "Now, let's talk about what we're about to do. Then, we can pick on Zane's lack of taste in women."

"Hey!" Skylar yelped as a piece of now-cold toast hit Jace right between the eyes, thrown by her, of course. Ah, how he loved his life.

Jace just hoped this wasn't the last day of it.

That would fucking suck.

CHAPTER FIFTEEN

"So, you and Zane, huh?"

Jace was sitting behind the wheel of the rental car as Skylar sat beside him in the passenger seat. Zane was busy getting the modified Go-Pro camera with its attached cable ready to record everything about to take place. Franklin and Alex were speaking a few yards away, their heads with their brilliant brains close to raise the confidence level to break through their worry. Kitt sat on the shore of the water and Jace knew she hated everything about this, biding her time to be done and over with this so they could go home tomorrow.

"I know, it's crazy or at least *as* crazy as all of this, Jace." She sat back and closed her eyes as a hand came up to press against her forehead. "It just happened. I have no idea why or how, but it did. I would love to say it was a liquor fueled one-night stand, but I wasn't drunk. Tipsy, yes, but to the point where my logic wouldn't be in the way to fuck Zane? No." She turned her head to look at him to give a rare glimpse of the vulnerability he knew she strived, almost obsessively, to hide. "I wish I could explain it, because then I could train myself to not allow it to happen again."

She brought her hand down to inspect her nails as a deep frown formed on her forehead. "It's like I had blinders on when it came to Zane. I wasn't seeing the whole scope of the man. Just the irritating, aggravating, and annoying parts of him in that limited view. But he's far deeper than I realized." She snorted in slight amusement. "Do you want to talk about how intense he is in bed next?" She turned her head to give him a nervous smile. "He, unlike you, checked out my ass as well as the rest of my attached parts and had sex with me. He, most definitely, is not a man I have to ask if he's gay or not."

Jace laughed at that reference back to the early times of their friendship when Sky had serious doubts of his heterosexual status. Apparently, a long history of being hit on by every male she had ever met set-up the bafflement when he had not. "He's always been deep. And no, please do not tell me your critique of his sexual prowess. Don't make me regret I brought the topic up, Sky." Reaching out, he took her hand and brought it up to his lips to kiss the knuckles. "I think it's good for both of you. Pretty sure it's not completely selfish to want all my friends as happy as I am." Giving her a smile, he brought their clasped hands to his chest and exhaled slowly as he swung his gaze to Kitt on the shore. She could have been a statue. Carved out of the same stone that sat around her at the water's edge. "Speaking of."

Exiting the car, he walked over to his girlfriend and sat next to her. Staring at her face for a moment, he then wrapped his arm around her as his eyes went to the cold, grey-blue of the lake in front of them. "It's huge. I see why it's called a Great Lake." He turned his head to press his lips against the side of her head. "Talk to me, baby. I need to know that you're not going to…" His words halted because he was once again struck with the fact that the woman he held carried his child. "I need to know this isn't going to panic you too much. It's more important now than ever."

He felt Kitt's exhale and she angled herself to meet his eyes. "You mean now that I'm pregnant? Will that change you doing this? Stop it all and we just go back to the hotel, cuddle, make plans for a nursery in the beach house? Pick out colors? Make a gift list? Try to control Sky's laser focus on taking charge of a baby shower? She already made a Target wish list." Her blue eyes searched his intensely before her long lashes fluttered to meet her cheeks. "No. We both know it won't. But Jace…" she rose to her feet and crossed her arms in a protective manner over her stomach. "I'll do my best to stay calm. To handle this. But if you truly care about this baby. Even if our love isn't enough, you'll make this the last time. I won't have a child, our baby, ever wonder if daddy is going to be dead and never coming home. If helping a stranger is more important than coming home to us." She looked back at him as she lifted her chin. "I can't watch you do this. I'm sorry. I just can't. I'm going to wait in the other car. And please don't ask me to."

And before Jace could tell her he wouldn't, she left him sitting there and walked away.

"Remember, you can't deny your body's impulse to react to drowning. In fact, by your own instructions, you need to feel that panic like Amanda did, correct?"

Jace nodded. "Right. If this is going to fucking work, I have to. She did, so yeah."

The temperature outside hovered right about freezing and the water a few degrees below that. A key to survival rested on Jace experiencing hypothermia. A body's biological protection against someone drowning in freezing climates. Franklin talked his way through assurances and the plan in order to calm Jace—or perhaps to calm himself. Jace wasn't sure. He only wore light clothes and no jacket. The cold day already had his teeth chattering and had him shivering with each nod to Franklin's instructions.

"Right. How long do you think that will take? After I uh," Jace swallowed, "drown?" He tried to force his eyes from staring at the lake beyond the hood of the car. It looked cold and if Zane's research was correct, just deep enough at the end of the boat ramp to allow the vehicle to become completely submerged, but not enough to prevent them from freeing him from its confines. He knew they had covered every single detail, but right now all his mind could process was that he was about to drown. He was going to struggle. And then by either saving grace or a perfect plan, hypothermia would prevent him from death.

Franklin's palm pressed down on Jace's shoulder and the contact enabled Jace to force his focus to the man. The older man's eyes behind those John Lennon glasses held calmness, understanding, and wisdom. Franklin kept his voice calm and informative. "You will hit the water and it only takes minutes for hypothermia to take ahold. The first stage is the cold shock response. It will affect your breathing. You'll start to gasp, perhaps hyperventilate, as your body responds to the sudden drop of your core temperature. Panic, which of course is also a response, will hasten this stage, but it normally passes quickly to the next stage."

Zane started stacking bags of ice next to Franklin on the ground by the opened passenger door. Jace's eyes jerked to it, but Franklin's soothing, almost monotone voice brought him back. "The second stage is cold incapacitation and usually, that comes about as soon as the five-minute mark. Your body will do what it can to conserve what little body heat remains through vasoconstriction. A fancy word," the man gave a shaky smile, "where your body restricts and decreases blood flow to your arms, legs, everywhere but your vital organs to protect them. You will lose movement of your hands, feet, arms, and legs." Jace looked at the floats attached to his arms and the ring around his neck. They needed hypothermia to hit before he drowned.

"Then, hypothermia sets in. Violent shivering. Slow and shallow breathing. Confusion. And you'll feel incredibly exhausted. You won't be able to speak and if you do, it will be slurred a great deal. Then, your pulse will go very weak…"

Jace nodded once again. "And then I drown." His eyes went back to the lake at that thought. The floats they had secured had been tested. A slow enough leak to keep him at that stage for 15 minutes as his body shut down, but not so much to not keep him afloat once it had.

"Hey guys. Sorry," Jace turned his head to see Zane standing there in the driver's door. "I got to get this hooked up. We got maybe forty-five minutes of low traffic before the school down the road lets out. Some may try to go around the detour and past here." Zane held the Go-Pro camera inside of a waterproof case used for underwater diving but Zane had taken an additional step of wiring in a cable so they could watch the footage live at the ramp. The videoing of it all had been Jace's idea. He was on a learning curve with all of this. He wanted to be able to watch it later. After all, they had seen the demons in the water previously by using a kiddy pool in Jace's bedroom—who's to say they wouldn't be able to see Amanda's if he found them? He wanted to make sure.

Alex had been completely supportive of that as well as Franklin—they could monitor him better that way. Alex hoped it would assist them in the research of Jace's unknown powers. It was all wish, hope, and maybe when it came to any component of the supernatural elements—but it was all they had at this point.

Franklin reached over Jace to lay that calming palm on Zane, who was less of a talker and more of a doer when nervous. Jace watched as his friend secured the electronics and he urged Franklin to continue. "What next? You said there was a fourth, final stage. Something about a mystery to medical knowledge?" Jace laughed harshly as he dropped his head back against the rest to look at the holistic healer and modern-day druid. "I know you love talking about that mystical, magical mumbo-jumbo shit. What's it called?"

Franklin gave another one of those smiles. "The circum-rescue collapse. It's not understood why it happens or what triggers it. You will not be conscious or shouldn't be. It's at that point where we have to make sure to rescue you. Warm your system with the IV fluids and warming blankets. Alex and I will have both ready the moment we pull you out. Compressions to remove the water. Rescue breathing, if needed. We brought the portable defibrillator, but I don't believe we'll need it." Franklin had voiced concern about Jace's heart withstanding such a measure. It was still healing from the last time it had stopped and been restarted. That fear glimmered in the man's eyes for a brief second to contradict the words as Franklin patted Jace's shoulder and moved out of the car.

"Zane." The man's head was down, uncoiling the coaxial cable that ran from the camera, now secured to the car's dash. "Zane, listen, there's something I want to say."

Zane shook his head and stiffened, but refused to look up. "Don't want to hear it, dude. You're going to be fine. Don't get all mushy and bromance-y and crap, okay?"

Jace laughed a bit. "Fine, I won't. And fuck, of course I'm going to survive, I got the Dead Man Crew making sure of that. But what I have to say is about Skylar."

Zane looked up then, the coil of cable stilled in shaking fingers. "Look, I know it's a surprise even to me and her. But I've had a thing for her for a while. I didn't act on it before, because I thought you two would hook up. Have you met you? You've got that whole smoldering, brooding anti-hero mojo going on. Girls can't resist that."

Jace found himself chuckling at that. "Yeah, she always wondered why we didn't hook-up too. I just never thought of her that way. Still don't. Never will. She's too good of a friend and I have Kitt now. But it's not that."

He cupped his hands on one of his best friends' face in order to look deep into Zane's eyes. His tone as serious as he could muster. He strived to match the gravity of this moment between them. "I have to know…was she really good in bed?" He then cracked a huge smile at Zane's reaction and actually pulled off a laugh. "I'm kidding. Lighten up. I'm not about to die and stay that way while I have a baby on the way. Can you believe that? I'm going to be a father."

Zane sputtered, not recovering as fast as normal and pointed a finger in Jace's face, but a smile showed in spite of the current dire situation. "Dude, not cool. Not even close to cool. Which is ironic since my ass is sitting on bags of ice."

But Jace was relieved to see the tactic succeeded. Zane's hands no longer shook and his friend's rigid, nervous stance appeared looser. Completing the video set up, Zane bent down to say, voice edged with wicked delight, "She was great in bed. But she had a great surfer to ride her waves." The man then did a hang-ten gesture with his hand and moved out of the car door opening.

And began to pack in the ice.

"Kitt, they're about to start."

Skylar had followed Kitt from the lakeshore and found her friend curled up in the backseat with ear buds in place. Sky heard pop music blasting from Kitt's phone playlist and waited until she heard a pause between tracks. "Are you sure you don't want to go down there?"

Kitt shook her head as Skylar joined her in the backseat of the primary rental for the trip. Not the second one, about to take her friend and Kitt's boyfriend and father of her child, into the depths of Lake Erie to drown.

"I can't Sky. I just can't. I don't want to see it. Hear it. I want to just pretend I'm waiting for him to show up from another business trip." She lifted her eyes to meet her friend's as she slowly removed the earpieces. "Like normal couples. Thrilled to have him home and pretending I didn't miss him as much as he knows I really did." She brought a hand up and wiped away her tears in evident frustration. "You think he knows how much I wish we were *that* couple instead of one facing off demons and death? He's smart. I'm sure he does and that makes me feel like shit, Sky." She covered her face with her hands. "He's out there, facing down death and I'm being the shittiest girlfriend in the history of girlfriends."

Sky moved to close the car door and listened as Kitt sobbed, each word from her friend tugging at her heart. Sure, it was hard as fuck being Jace's bestie in this, but Sky had no idea how hard it must have been to be in Kitt's relationship shoes with the man. To think she had been angry at her when she left the hotel the other day—talk about feeling like shit. "Maybe he knows that. But Kitt, no one should have to face what you're having to with all of this. And now, being pregnant and dealing?" Skylar reached out to put her hand on Kitt's drawn up knee. "I can't even imagine. It's bad enough for me and I'm not in love with him. Having a baby with him. I don't think any of us could judge you for how you're handling it. And I apologize for doing that before. I suck as a friend."

Kitt laughed a sad sound and again wiped her tears. "You're right. How dare you introduce me to the man I love more than life itself." She snorted. "Apparently and literally on the life part since he seems to like to die. If you hadn't done that, I would be more miserable than I am now." She paused and couldn't help but let out a weak laugh. "Well, not as miserable as I am right now, but you know what I mean." She sucked her bottom lip between her teeth and looked back through the rear windshield towards the car and the lake beyond. "He has to survive this, Sky. I can't even think of a single next step without him in it. Not just for this baby," her head ducked forward and down as her hand went to her stomach, "but a life. One without him in it. It's strange, but in such a short time, he's become such a part of my life that I don't want to remember what it was like without him."

Skylar pulled Kitt into a hug and together they held each other. Both of them were crying and most likely, they were exchanging snot tee-to-tee, but Skylar didn't care. When she felt Kitt's sobbing ease, she said between her own, "I can't believe you're going to have a baby with him."

Kitt laughed, full of sniffles laced with hic-cups from crying so hard. "And I can't believe you screwed Zane."

Both women were laughing now, wiping each other's tears, and Skylar found a box of courtesy Kleenex in the center console. "Here. Blow your nose. Wipe your tears and go kiss your man, Kitt. He's scared. He's covering it, but he's so scared. This is still so unknown to him. But he's so amazing to want to help others. We're just so selfish that we want him all to ourselves." She held her friend's face between her hands. "But that also makes him a superhero. And what baby mama doesn't want one of those in her life?"

Jace tried to slow his breathing and remain calm. Any minute, he would get a motion from Zane at the car's front fender to floor the gas pedal. Jace felt like screaming. Zane jerked to stand stiff suddenly and Jace thought they had been busted.

The driver's door was suddenly pulled open and Kitt's face appeared in the space in front of him. Jace could not fight with her right now. He needed to focus on the collective detailed insanity of the plan. "Kitt, I have to do…"

"I know. I know you do. And I still can't watch. But there was no way I was letting you do this without telling you how much I love you. How amazing you are to do this. Even if I *hate it,* I know you must do it. It's why you are who you are. And I'm so proud of you." She gave him a smile with tears coursing down her cheeks, as she took one of his hands, which shook violently from all the ice around him, and placed it on her stomach. "We're so proud of you. And we'll be waiting. In another car." She brought her lips to his and smiled against them. "The one that's warm. And not in the water."

They both laughed and then she kissed him. It was so blisteringly warm due to him being so cold. His soul drank up the warmth to use as a buoy inside to float calm above his anxiety. He brought his free hand up to cup against her cheek, absorbing her heat as much as he could. Their eyes met as she pulled back. "I love you too.

Both of you. And keep that car running, so I can warm up my freezing feet on you when I get back."

Kitt crinkled up her nose in that adorable way he had cherished from day one. "So, basically the same as every night when you come to bed." She laughed again and they kissed. This time when she broke the contact, she rested her forehead on his as she looked into Jace's eyes. "See you soon."

He nodded and whispered back, "You too. See you soon."

Zane was telling them it was time to go, but god did Jace hate it when Kitt stepped back and the door was closed, leaving him alone once again. Looking back, teeth chattering so hard he thought he might pop a filling, he watched Skylar lead Kitt back to the other car and then faced forward.

"Let's go find some fucking water demons and go home," he snarled, as he brought up a thumbs up, matted the gas pedal, and the car took off towards the lake.

CHAPTER SIXTEEN

"Fuck! It's cold," he said, because it was. The car hit the water harder than Jace anticipated, but luckily, the air bags did not engage. Maybe Zane had factored that in and disabled them prior, but Jace hadn't thought to ask. Water rushed in thanks to the brilliant idea of leaving the rear windows down, so the ass end of the car went faster under water while the front stayed level with its surface—for now. His eyes went to the timer that had been lodged in the Go-Pro case in front of him.

Fifteen seconds that felt like minutes. His feet and legs were already going numb, as the front of the vehicle tilted and began to fill. Several of the bags of ice had broken loose of their cheap plastic and cubes of the stuff floated around him as the water reached his waist. They tapped against him, as if to remind him he was going to feel as frozen as they were very soon. Like Jace could possibly forget that fact.

Thirty seconds and he was shivering so hard, that his back ached from the violence of it. And try as he might to not fight, he started to. Frantically, he tried to undo the seat belt buckle but found duct tape there. "Wait! Stop. This was *stupid!*" His hands went out to cup around the Go-Pro. "Is this thing working?! I said stop! I changed my fucking mind! Can you hear me?! Zane!" But they had planned for this as they had the rest—ignore him and do not stop—even if he begged. Jace had made that clear in the instructions.

Fifty seconds and the water swirled around his chest. He became unable to speak as his breath went fast, hyperventilating, and his heart pounded at what felt like an impossible pace to maintain and not tear apart.

Sixty seconds and Jace's breathing leveled out. The gasping eased as the water rose to his shoulders. His eyes locked on the timer counting down the time as he brought a hand up. It shook so bad, it was almost impossible to do and he gave a thumbs up.

"How's he doing?" Alex paced behind Zane and Franklin as they watched the live feed from the car that slipped morbidly gracefully into the water of the cold lake. She stopped to stand behind the two men once the car disappeared under the surface with just a few inches of the car's roof above.

Franklin did not look up, but watched a stopwatch that was synced with the timer inside the submerged vehicle. "He made it through stage one." He chuckled as he told her about Jace's thumbs up moments before. "We're three minutes in. Stage two should begin. That's when his body should change his blood flow to his organs. We'll know it has when he can no longer move."

Zane, whose focus was on the tablet held in his hands, chanced a glance over at Franklin. "He's just shaking. Talking to himself. Well, I think he's talking to himself." Zane hit the volume control on the Go-Pro and they all heard what Jace was saying. "Baby names. Is he saying baby names?" Zane looked up at Alex in disbelief. "He was freaking earlier. But it settled down. I guess baby planning isn't that hard of a tactic to go to. Shit and fuck me, this is harder than I thought."

Franklin patted Zane's knee and Alex moved to sit down next to him. "Incapacitation is next. How much longer Frankie?"

Franklin turned his head her way and held up the stopwatch to show five minutes. "Now. It should be now."

"Cassie. Short…for…Cassandra. But I like…Cas too. If… it's a girl…" But suddenly without warning, Jace lost the ability to move his mouth and whisper. His hands dropped as if they had gone to sleep. The tingling, pin-and-needles sensation stabbing through him was more painful than if he had sat or laid wrong. He wanted to scream but it was as if he was paralyzed. The water was now under his chin and the floatie around his neck, which had assisted to keep his head above the water, was barely doing its duty now due to deflation. His arms, the floaties flat and useless, sank below the water as if they were disconnected. Human arm shaped pool noodles rather than attached and living body parts.

His eyes, the only parts capable of movement, jerked to the timer as it hit ten minutes. Ice cubes now clung to him, finding kindred in the freezing. Jace could make out one stuck to his face near his right eye. The water was right beneath that and he felt a frenzied panic rise within him. Jace couldn't do shit to ease its claim. It had no intention of lessening. His heart beat loudly. He expected to see the liquid around him pulse with it, but no. The water was lazy and easing up, inch-by-inch.

Oh fuck, what the hell was I thinking… I'm going to die as a frozen fucking idiot…

"What is that?"

Alex was watching the live feed as something strange appeared in the water. "Is that what I think it is?"

Both Franklin and Zane gave the tablet's video feed their full attention. Zane tapped the screen and shrugged. "Has to be the damn Go-Pro shorting out. Shit, it's supposed to be good to go up to a thousand feet deep."

Franklin took the tablet from Alex and shook his head. "No. That's not the camera." He threw the tablet to her as he got to his feet. "It looks like black frost. How can it be possible *in* water? It has to be demons!" Franklin ran towards the ramp.

Alex had learned one thing about the supernatural unknowns of the world. The impossible was only that until it wasn't. She watched helplessly on the tablet as the water went over Jace's head and he stopped moving.

"Wait, what? Oh shit!" Zane yelped in alarm as he rose to run after the older man. "Stay here!" Apparently, Zane wanted Franklin out of the way and he was the strongest swimmer on the crew. Zane reached the water's edge at the end of the boat ramp and dove into its freezing depths.

Alex caught up with Franklin and together, they stood there at the edge, unable to see anything in the murky water. Ice cubes had bobbed up, but no sign of Jace. "Franklin, does that mean the demons found him? How? He's not in the nightmare realm yet, is he? What is going on?!"

"I don't know, Alex." He met her eyes and grabbed her hand desperately. She looked down at the video still playing and let out a frightened gasp—they could no longer see. Black frost or *something* had covered their view.

CHAPTER SEVENTEEN

Jace was in a box made of thick, seamless glass and about the size of his bedroom in the beach house. Surrounding it was water and he turned slowly to observe ice cubes, all perfectly square and opaque as they tapped against the outer walls. His last recalled thought had been him drowning and unable to move. Screaming internally, being unable to perform it externally. And now, without a warning, he stood inside of this new form of entrapment.

Moving his hands, he frowned to see there was a fluid inside of the box as well. But it was thicker, swirling as he moved his fingers and here, there was no drowning. "Because I'm dead. Again," he muttered as he turned. The movements felt slower due to the pressure of the liquid—he imagined it would be like being encapsulated within clear syrup. Like an insect becoming trapped in sap. An organism dropped into a cube of melting glycerin and unable to escape.

Behind him was a vehicle and Jace recognized it from the Bishops' car wreck. The same one he found himself in previously when he tried to reach Amanda.

Walking against the resistance of the fluid around him, he bent down to see that the car was empty this time. No sign of Amanda or her husband, Steven.

"You're wrong…"

The words came from behind. Their sound garbled. Spoken and somehow, heard through the goop. Looking over his shoulder, Jace found Amanda sitting there—not there before—in her wheelchair. She was wearing a hospital gown with ankles strapped to the footrests and wrists strapped to the armrests. Facing her, he narrowed his eyes and looked around him before addressing her. Was it Amanda? Or was it a demon? He knew better than to accept anything in the alternate realm at face value. Nothing…was ever as it appeared. "Amanda, what do you mean I'm wrong? Explain."

She began to struggle. Jace stepped forward, that odd fluid resistance disorienting but so far, not causing any issue and squatted down in front of her. "Amanda, calm down. I want to help you. But I need you to explain how I'm wrong. I need more information. Can you give that to me?"

Suddenly, her face contorted, each vein and capillary pulsing and going dark under her too pale, almost white skin. Her mouth went grotesque with a scream—its size impossibly long to have a jaw made of bone. The lower half stretched to her chest. The screeching from her throat was inhuman and at such a pitch that Jace stumbled back to protectively put his hands over his ears. The waves vibrated in the liquid surrounding them. Like a tuning fork on glass.

"Stop!" He screamed. She did. Only to replace it with thrashing and wails of desperation. Risking a step forward, Jace placed his hands on the armrests on either side of the chair and came in close. "Tell me how I can help you move on. How I can release you from the demons, Amanda. Please."

She sobbed and her tears were ice as they fell, clinking on the floor like chimes made of winter. She angled herself forward and whispered in a voice full of fear, "You are wrong. You are wrong. You are wrong!"

"Wrong how!?" Jace roared. He refused to back away again. "How am I wrong?!"

She went still and came even closer and smiled. "Not my demons."

Suddenly, the watery light surrounding the cube darkened. Amanda started laughing and Jace spun away. Something had joined the ice cubes outside the box. Dark and sinister as it swirled and took form. There were dozens of them. Black tendrils floating like fish made of some primordial, living phantasmal ink. They swam almost leisurely around the box as Amanda's laughter went hysterically insane.

Jace observed their new company and the woman went silent and still. He reached a wall and placed his hand against the glass. The dark shapes followed his movement. Some even nudged yet closer to his touch, but the wall between them prevented it. He was fascinated by their fixation as he trailed his hand downward only to find a thin trickle of a different liquid swirling at his feet. Red. Thicker than water…

Jace glanced backwards over his shoulder and watched in horror as each letter of his last name cut through on Amanda's throat. Blood ran from first the "C", then the "A." He lost his frantic footing in the blood and landed on his ass as the "M" appeared. His back hit the car behind him. The paralysis from drowning returned to imprison Jace here—unable to move or look away. Forced to watch in fascinated horror at the gory forming of his name.

Behind Amanda, the behavior of the ink demons changed. They started to slam against the exterior glass walls and more appeared, driven into some sort of feeding frenzy. Bizarre sharks, as more of Amanda's blood hit the floor. The moment his name was complete, the ability to move returned as he rose to his feet. The cuts of letters were so deep that only a few tendons and stretches of skin remained. Somehow,

Amanda started that screeching again. Completely, totally fucking impossible considering her throat no longer existed in the carnage that was her neck.

The ink demons grew frenzied, their strikes against the box's glass walls harder. The thuds were a calliope of noise—thud, thud, thud, thud. Scream, scream. It was nothing compared to the more sickening thud as Amanda's head ripped free and hit the floor with a squishing, solid sound. As if its impact was the catalyst to the cube's integrity, the walls cracked and the water with the demons started pouring in. The school swam through the liquid, still reminding Jace more of sharks when he caught sight of rows of razor teeth.

Especially when they attacked.

He was bloody chum. A meal too tempting not to eat.

"Hey! What's going on here?"

Alex turned to see a city worker from the roads department had pulled up and was now out of his truck to yell at them. She grabbed Franklin's arm and they both turned to stop the man from advancing with their previously practiced alibis.

"A car! It drove into the lake!" She pointed back as Zane stumbled up the boat ramp, dragging Jace out of the water. "We're doctors. Can you get us help?" That too was part of the plan—the better safe than sorry portion.

The worker looked from her and Franklin to Zane with Jace. "Oh shit! I'm calling it in." He ran back to his truck. Alex ran back to drop to her knees next to Jace as Franklin ran to their car to get the gear. Darting a look at Zane, Alex gave him an encouraging touch on the arm.

"You did good. But you might want to hide all that." She tilted her chin towards the tablet and the cable connected Go-Pro camera that lay on the boat ramp.

Zane was soaking wet but not completely freaked out. "I got it and the duct tape out of the car when I grabbed him." He met her eyes. "The whole car was covered in that black frost, goo shit and it kept me from getting the doors open. If we hadn't left the back windows opened. Alex…" He swallowed and now the fear appeared. "I wouldn't have been able to." He glanced up as Kitt and Skylar ran towards them and he rose on shaky legs to put away the video gear.

"Oh my god, baby!" Kitt knelt by Jace's head and met Alex's eyes. "Is he… please tell me…"

Franklin had arrived. Alex replied to Kitt's worry using the only facts she was sure of in the moment as she pressed her fingers against Jace's neck. "He has a shallow pulse. He's alive." She turned Jace on his side and worked at getting the needle into his arm to administer the warm saline. Franklin tucked the warmed blankets around Jace. Both kept warm in the thermal bag they had been stored in the car.

"First, we the get the water out of his lungs. Second, we get him warm. Third, we get him conscious." Alex's focus split for a second as the sounds of sirens ripped through the otherwise eerily quiet air. "He'll be fine. We need to just to do as we planned. He'll be fine." Alex knew the tight tremble in her tone and the shaking of her hands didn't offer comfort to Jace's girlfriend. But she was doing her best.

Both an ambulance and police cruiser parked next to the city worker's truck. Alex said low to Skylar, who knelt next to Kitt, "Sky, looks like the expected response has arrived. Let's just hope it goes as we planned." The woman gave a quick nod, hugged Kitt, and then rose to meet the authorities. "Please let this all work. I really do not want to learn if Orange is The New Black," Alex whispered.

"His pulse is stronger. It's working," Franklin said with a gentle hand squeeze to hers.

Proof of that came when Jace started coughing. He spewed water on the pavement by his head. Alex resisted a fist bump of victory. That would have made the cover of her and Franklin being strangers taking photos of the lake vulnerable. It was thin-skinned as it stood, without her doing the job of the police by shooting holes into it.

Franklin rolled Jace to his back and Alex let out an exhale of relief when Jace's hazel eyes were cracked open. Although bloodshot and full of confusion, she welcomed the sight. He shivered and his teeth chattered together so hard she could hear the sound. "Take it easy, Jace. You're here."

Alex laid a hand on his forehead and bent down to whisper, "And so are the police and EMTs." She gave a side-eye glance as the emergency responders approached. Skylar had deftly intercepted the police officer. "Hopefully, you can remember our plan?"

Jace gave her a weak nod. Alex smiled as she bent lower to whisper in his ear, "Dead Man Crew engaged." Moving back to her haunches, she let out a slow exhale and closed her eyes in order to organize her brain along with her façade. She then rose to her feet to intercept the men before they reached Jace.

"I'm Doctor Alex Martinez. And this is my boyfriend, Franklin Wormwood. We came to take pictures of the lake and this man's car went into the lake!" She angled her body to the side to allow the EMTs to view Jace but impeded their advance. "I believe the woman is his girlfriend and the other, a friend? I don't know really. But I heard the three of them arguing and next thing we know..."

She added a laugh and her hands waved around to block more attempts to do their jobs. "Vroom! The man must have hit the wrong gear and there went his car!" The nervous laugh seemed natural even if the lies were not. "I've never seen anything like it, have you, Honey?"

Franklin put an arm around Alex and shrugged. "Nor I, Honeybee. Not in my life." The men finally maneuvered around them and she hoped they had bought Jace enough time. She whispered to Franklin as they followed, "Honeybee? Really? A bit too much, Frankie, don't you think?"

His face crinkled with a slight smile in spite of the trepidation regarding the outcome of all this. He bent down with the premise of kissing the side of Alex's head and whispered in reply, "I have not ever seen a man purposely drive into a cold lake. The truth is always best utilized when one can, Alexis. And honeybees are both a threatened species and amazing creatures. Much like you, my dear."

Alex stumbled over her own feet at the shock of Franklin's words. Did he just flirt with her?

CHAPTER EIGHTEEN

Kitt chewed on the nail of a finger on one hand, while her other hand clung tight to Jace's. The ambulance brought them to the local emergency room. The police had filed a report. The crew's story not questioned. No additional inquiry as to what happened. Zane's research of time and location being best for no witnesses was correct. The police officers told them people drove into the lake often. That fact helped and the authorities considered the incident closed.

Jace passed out before they could load him into the ambulance. His body temperature reached normal on the way to the emergency room. His heart, however, took longer to stabilize. An hour had gone by and Kitt was worried. With the exception of jerks and mumbles, Jace gave no sign of coming to. Only one person was allowed to go back with him, but Kitt answered multiple texts from the crew as they waited anxiously in the waiting room.

She had just replied to another one when suddenly, Jace bolted up and yelled hoarsely, "Not her demons!" He then proceeded to thrash as if to escape something other than the bed.

"Hey, baby. It's okay. You're at the hospital. It's fine." She cupped his face in her hands. It took a few seconds for his eyes to focus on hers and the absolute terror Kitt found there made her pull him close. She wrapped her arms around him as she climbed into the bed with him. "Shh, you're not in that realm anymore. I have you, Jace. I'm here. Just calm down, okay?" Her eyes went to the monitors in concern after seeing his heart-rate jump dangerously high when he woke. The blinking red indictor started to slow as she rocked him. Her hand moved over his back and found his muscles quivered with a few spastic jerks. She knew Jace always struggled after these events to solidify the connection of life and reality, while severing the link from dead and nightmare.

Kitt pulled back just enough so she could see him and brushed her fingers through his damp hair, where a cold sweat slicked its strands and her fingers. "What did you mean just now? Do you remember?" She lowered her voice as a nurse walked in to check the monitors, only to leave them alone once more. "You said something about 'not her demons?' Amanda's? Did you see them?"

Jace was forced to lay back as a fit of coughing hit. Kitt raised the head of the bed to assist and get him more comfortable. He reached to keep her close and tugged on her hand to return. Kitt happily complied by curling against him. She placed a hand on his chest and splayed her fingers to rest over his heart. She steeled herself not to look at the monitor to sync with the beat she felt under her palm.

As the rise and fall of his chest leveled out without coughing, she lifted her eyes up as he spoke.

"She said I was wrong. And she said it was *my* demons. She didn't have any."

Kitt frowned deeply, her nose crinkling as she tried to understand what Jace meant. "What do you mean she didn't have any?" She jerked up to sit in alarm. "Wait, did you see the bitch that attached to Laura?"

Jace shook his head. "No. She didn't have any. Not a single one. They were outside of where Amanda's soul is trapped. But…" His eyes skidded around the room and his forehead creased in thought. "It wasn't until I tried to help that they got in. A different…" He squeezed his eyes shut. Kitt knew he tried to not only recall but organize what he witnessed in the nightmare realm. Unfortunately, Jace learned his soul warrior powers did not hinder the mind's habit to forget details of a nightmare the more awake it became. Kitt would often find Jace, fresh from nightmares and covered in sweat, jotting down notes in a notebook he kept by their bed. Capturing even the smallest details before they faded.

"Different type of demon." He brought a hand up to knead his brows. "They wanted…."

He seemed more confused with each word. Kitt was afraid he tried too much, too soon. "Jace, maybe you need to rest." She pressed her lips against his. "I mean, it's not like you didn't just drown and we're sitting in an emergency room."

If only it was that easy. It never was with Jace Camden. He must have been a starving terrier denied a bone in a previous incarnation. When his unique mind grabbed onto a theory, there was no tearing him away from it. Normally, Kitt enjoyed and made humor of it. But she could swear she felt cold, dead breath teasing the nape of her neck since they had pulled Jace out of the lake. A frozen residue somehow transferred from the man she loved to her. She felt frozen from the inside out and her humor with it.

"They wanted me, Kitt. Not Amanda. Me." He made an effort to stand and Kitt moved off the bed to stand in front to stop him. His eyes darted around. Lips pressed together with intensity of thought. She brought her hands up to cup his face. When his gaze came to hers, the churning emotions she found were sharply jarring and turbulent. Her Jace was scared.

"What do you mean? They were in her nightmares, but they were *your* demons? Or her demons, but they weren't with her?" It was her turn to bring a hand up against her forehead. "Baby, you're not making much sense. I didn't think that's how it worked. Her demons would be with her soul. How are your demons there?"

"I don't know!" The yell startled Kitt. She had gotten used to the strong emotions that sometimes burst from Jace without warning, a normal occurrence when he felt overwhelmed or confused, and she did her best to not take it personally. But he rarely lashed out at her. She knew Jace was desperate to figure out what was going on and the guilt rose at the pressure she had added with her demands to go. If only there was a "How to be a Superhero's Girlfriend" book she could order from Amazon and get with free shipping the Prime way. Not that she had checked. And not that she wouldn't see if such a book did exist later.

"Okay, okay, baby." Kitt pulled him into a hug and pressed her cheek against his chest and focused on his heartbeat again. Each rise and fall of his chest, his breathing ragged with frustration. "So, what does this mean?" She lifted his chin in order to meet his eyes. "Are we still leaving tomorrow?"

Jace's focus shifted to the wall behind her. Kitt could tell that he ground his teeth. She felt his jaw tensing with it under her palm. He was considering both the question and how to answer it. After a silent minute, the jaw movement ceased and she felt the tension loosen ever so slightly. His gaze shifted to hers.

"It's my demons. Amanda said I was wrong. My trying brings more of them to her." He let out a hard, body-shaking exhale. "I can fight my own demons. I don't need to be here to do that." Kitt couldn't help the sigh of relief at his concession. He brought his forehead to meet hers and added, "We're going home."

CHAPTER NINETEEN

"Maybe you should have stayed at the hospital? We could have rescheduled the flights."

Alex meant well with her words. She was concerned for him as were the rest of the Dead Man's Crew. They said something similar last night when he left the emergency room. He had to sign a waiver to even be allowed to leave the hospital against medical advice.

Kitt, too, was concerned but not once suggested they stay. Jace knew she wanted to leave as soon as possible. Afterall, she hadn't been a fan of this "adventure" in Ohio since day one.

The concerns continued this morning, but Jace was firm in his belief there was nothing more they could do here. He wasn't allowed to see Amanda. Even without taking that into consideration, Alex had let him know that Amanda would be moved to her home under hospice care tomorrow. Jace hoped that now that he was aware of the new twisted games the demons played to kill him, they would allow the woman to die in peace.

As he packed his duffel, Kitt hugged him from behind, her arms going around him and her face pressed against his back. He needed that affirming touch. Torn emotionally from walking away from whatever the fuck this was. To leave without knowing without a doubt that Amanda would be free. If the tragedy of his late wife's suicide taught Jace one thing, it was that death was never simple. It dug in its ruthless claws; sank in merciless, feasting fangs to suck a soul dry even after life released its claim.

A nagging worry seeded that not only would his soul be payment like it had been with Laura but Kitt's. And now a baby.... Jace turned in Kitt's embrace and his eyes went to her belly as he placed a hand on over its flatness. They had months but if Jace knew one thing, it was time was never his friend. There was far more to lose now than there had ever been. He would not risk a soul barely formed.

"Baby, we're fine."

Kitt's soft voice drew Jace out of his thoughts. He found her eyes so full of fucking love for him. Jace had every reason to walk away from this. To demand some fucking happiness. Not only for a woman he barely knew but for his own damn self. For him, Kitt, and their baby. "Yeah. I'm going to make sure it stays that way too." He tilted her chin up and brought his mouth down to hers to mesh in a promise blended with a kiss.

"Hey, I'm taking our stuff down. You guys ready?" Zane's intrusion broke their moment. Kitt chuckled softly as she tucked her head under his chin, her soft hair tickling his three-day old beard scruff. "Oh sorry, were you two about to have sexy time ten-minutes short of check out?" Zane smiled mischievously as he snickered. "That's a record-breaking quickie. And fast recovery for a guy that had been dead yesterday." He moved towards Jace with a fist held out to bump. "But that's how you roll, right dude?"

Jace smirked and rather than make fist contact, he looped Kitt's bag over his friend's forearm. "Go. Take hers downstairs and get her some snacks. Grab some for Sky too. She's a royal bitch when she's hangry."

"I heard that!" jested Skylar as she walked past the open hotel room door with four pieces of luggage to everyone else's one. "But it is true." She paused and held her hand out to Kitt. "Come on, mommy and soon-to-be-spoiled nephew or niece by Auntie Skylar. Let's get snacks." She pointed a finger at Jace. "Grab his credit card for those. They have the really good Godiva boxes of chocolate in that shop in the lobby." She flashed Jace her most charming smile and dripped her tone with more southern drawl than normal. "Nothing says love for yo' bestie like expensive candy bought with someone else's plastic."

Kitt giggled but Jace could tell she was reluctant to let him go. Who could blame her after facing him dying in so many months? Jace was damn lucky she came back when she walked out a door. Many women would have stayed gone. "Go. I'll finish up here and meet you guys down there." She gave him a worried look and he smiled. "I can handle one bag with four pairs of clothes, undies, socks, and pajamas, baby." He called out to Skylar, who waited, "Unlike *some* people, I pack light." He cupped a palm against Kitt's cheek. "I love you. Go. And grab me a soda and chips while you're shopping."

"You sure?" Her voice held worry, but less now that they were leaving Ohio.

"Yeah. Completely. Go." He pulled out his wallet and handed it to her. "Just make sure Skylar doesn't have to draw up bankruptcy papers between now and when we get home." He rubbed noses with her and smiled when she said she loved him. After committing to hurry up and join them, the door closed and he was left alone in the room.

Checking the bathroom after retrieving his shaving kit, he tossed it down in the duffel bag and paused. Something caught his eye in the bottom of the bag. The flash drive. The one given to Alexis by Doctor Lewis.

Sitting on the end of the bed, Jace slowly rotated it in his fingers. Alex had presumed it held videos of Amanda's sessions. Jace wasn't sure it would reveal anything of use now. Why had Dr. Lewis thought anything on this drive would hold some clue to solving the mystery of Amanda Bishop's condition?

Curiosity getting the best of Jace, he tugged his laptop out of its travel sleeve in his duffel, booted it up, and put the drive in the USB slot. A file labeled "A. Bishop" contained MP4 format videos and he tapped the first one.

While it loaded, his phone lit up next to him with a received text from Kitt. *Doritos? Ranch or Nacho cheese?*

Jace could not stop the smile at such a mundane question. Perhaps it was because it was so fucking normal. He craved normalcy in his life every single day of his cursed existence. From childhood to now. He tapped a reply for her to pick. It didn't matter. Something flickering on his laptop screen caught his attention. The laptop was set to auto-play videos or else, he would have missed it.

"Wait…what the fuck?"

He stood holding the laptop in one hand while the other rewound the video. Jace watched intently as Steven Bishop entered the session room. Amanda was strapped to her wheelchair per protocol and appeared to be unresponsive. But there was something else. Jace zoomed and placed the laptop on the dresser. Bracing his arms stiffly on the furniture, he focused on the grainy black and white video from the closed-circuit camera at the facility. Noting the time stamp, he went back to watch as Steven leaned down and whispered something to his wife. Unfortunately, so quietly that Jace could not make out what was said. Whatever it was, it caused Amanda to jerk. A miniscule movement, but it was there.

What happened next had grabbed Jace's attention.

As Steven Bishop stood upright, something dark, shadowy, and moving stayed with Amanda. He had increased the volume to max in an effort to hear Bishop's whisper. Something sinister. A strange hissing sound Jace had come to think of as "demon whisper."

It hissed a single word.

The same word etching onto Amanda's exposed thigh as Jace watched.

Drawn with a finger formed by the shadow form Bishop left behind in the room.

C.A.M.D.E.N.

Jace hit pause and dumped out the laptop sleeve to find the printed photos sent to bring them here. They were printed still shots from the same video.

Two seconds after the demon had cut his name.

"How can you be sure?"

Jace had demanded them all to come back to the room. That led to mass confusion as to why. Check-out time had arrived and their flight home was scheduled to leave in two and a half hours. He now paced the hotel room as the others stood around the small table where the video he had seen played out to explain.

"Baby, we saw this already. This is what brought us here." She looked at him in worry. It wasn't too farfetched if she thought his drowning had caused some weird-ass stroke. "I don't see or hear anything."

"No! Those *photos* brought us here. *After* the demon carved my name. This we didn't see." Jace let out a frustrated growl and he stabbed a finger on the screen to hit rewind again. "You don't see that demon? The shadow shit? What about this…" He tried to turn up the volume beyond its highest level from before. "You don't *hear* that fucker saying my name? Right before *it* carves it in her skin? It wasn't her doing it. It's not her demon!" He gawked at the group. "How are you *not* seeing this shit?!"

Kitt, Sky, Franklin, and Alexis all stared at him. Zane softly whistled and decided the floor was a safer focus than Jace. Kitt moved to him and put her hands on his chest.

"No, baby. There's no demon. And I don't hear anything on that video." She moved her touch to his face. He angrily jerked away. They were treating him like a scraped knee toddler who only needed a fresh band-aid to fix a boo-boo.

Jace met her eyes and his lip curled off his teeth to hiss through them. "I see it. And just like all of you, I could not see it *or* hear it before. But now I do. It's fucking there." Pulling away from Kitt, he paced. "Remember how I couldn't see the demon feeding on Laura before? But once I did see it, in the pool, I was able to afterward? See it on others?" He paused to determine if they caught on, but nope.

He could have sprouted a second head and they would have believed *that* rather than the proof right in front of them. "You all could see it after you each had encounters, remember?" A flicker of understanding appeared on Franklin's face first. Jace grasped at it as he pointed a finger at the man. "You get it?"

Franklin stood, removed his glasses and wiped them with his shirt tail as he processed the information. "And since you saw them there with her." Glasses were put back in place. "What was it you called it?"

"Cube. It was a glass cube. Full of some thick liquid. Surrounded by water. Or at least I think it was water."

Franklin nodded and began to pace. "Yes, yes. The cube. Since you, shall we say, met the demons, you can now see them where you could not before." The older man then pointed at the others and brought the finger to his own chest. "And since we have not been introduced to those beings, we are not able to hear or see them. Correct?"

Jace let out a yelled, "Yes!" He may have done a fist pump, at the very least, figuratively. At least someone was starting to understand what he was saying. Otherwise he feared the nasty, past habit of considering himself insane reared its maniacal head again.

"Right." He scooped the printed photos off the table. "The demons weren't in these shots. And even if they were, I didn't *know* the demons yet. It wouldn't have mattered." He and Franklin gave each other a smile of synced thought processes. "I was just assuming it was *my* demons and not Amanda's. She didn't have any. She still doesn't."

"Her husband does!" Jace and Franklin exclaimed loudly in unison. Elated to have solved at least part of this fucked up mystery, they expressed the excitement with high-fives. Jace turned and expected to see the others had been brought along to the same excellent conclusion. Instead, he found baffled confusion.

And on Kitt's face—fear.

"Baby," he said softly, to lead into pleading for her to understand.

"But we're going home," Kitt said flatly as she rose to her feet. "You said we were going home. Our bags are downstairs in the lobby. We were going to get on the airport shuttle. To make our plane…with non-refundable tickets…to go home. In just two hours. Then in six hours, we would have been home."

Her voice took on a treble of betrayal. She moved to strike her hands against his chest and tears pooled at the edge of her lashes. "I want to go home, Jace. Take me home. Take me and our baby home." She lifted her chin to meet his eyes. "Now. You said," she started to cry, "we were going home." The sound of her defeat tore into Jace's thrill of revelation and replaced it with feeling like shit. Again.

Her hands balled into fists and slammed hard against his chest. "Tell me we are going home. You said we were *going home!*"

Jace pulled her into a hug. Not only to comfort, but also halt her onslaught. He rested his chin on the top of Kitt's head as she continued to struggle and sob. Her warm tears soaked into his shirt. He brought a hand up to comb fingers into her hair as lowered his mouth to her ear, each word catching as he whispered, "I can't go. Not yet. I'm sorry."

CHAPTER TWENTY

Kitt requested for Jace not to go with her to say goodbye at the airport. In fact, she had made the request through Skylar, because she didn't want to see or talk to him before she left. His girlfriend felt completely betrayed that he had broken his commitment for them to go home. He had tried to reach some sort of "meet-him-halfway" agreement. Stay for a few more days to validate that Steven Bishop hosted demons. That shot down, he desperately bargained for just one more day. Kitt had not been open to either suggestion. She wanted to go home and she was taking their baby with her. Jace dared not to point out there was no way she could leave without a womb. The bargaining was destined to fail in the face of her hurt and anger before it had even begun. But he had tried because shit…he hated hurting his beautiful Kitt.

There was no leaving until he tackled Amanda's situation with the information he now possessed. He had failed to save Laura before death and the demons took her from him. He would not let that happen to the woman now being tormented by the bastards, even if the woman he loved was solidly against him doing so. Jace would have to make it up to her in every way she allowed when he got home.

He was pretty sure Kitt would put an "if" in that statement rather than "when." Jace prayed she would not be proven right. There was zero comfort that he would be dead and unable to hear the "I told you so."

In the hotel room, rebooked for a few more days, Jace did not look up as Zane returned from taking the women to the airport. He had asked Skylar to please stay with Kitt. Alex needed to return to other patients with pending appointments. She did promise to assist Kitt as well.

Part of Jace ached with foolish hope that his girlfriend had changed her mind and would walk in with Zane. But no…the man returned alone. Oh well…hope had never been Jace's friend. Why should that history reverse itself now?

"What do we know?" he asked from where he sat on the bed, his laptop on his lap. He had watched all the clips from the flash drive. Only the one showed any demon activity. He had moved on to reading articles from local papers regarding the accident, followed by the police reports Skylar had pulled.

He glanced up to Zane and Franklin who regarded him with silence rather than input. Yeah, Kitt was not the only one upset about his choice to extend their stay. Sighing, he set the laptop to the side and crossed his arms. "I know. I hate that she left. I hurt her. She's upset and she's mad. But she's also safe at home. And the quicker we three figure out this fucked up mess, the faster I can get home and kiss her ass for forgiveness. Agreed?"

Zane snorted and pulled a piece of cold pizza from its box as he propped his sneakered feet on the end of the bed. "What I don't get is why Skylar is pissed at *me*. She said I was Team Jace and should be Team Skylar?" He took a bite of the pizza with a shrug. "Last I knew, we were a crew. The Dead Man's Crew. Not a team. When did we switch to teams? Did that happen and I wasn't told? Or does that happen when you have sex with a girl? It creates…shit, I don't know. Teams."

Zane, as he babbled, nervously devoured pizza. Franklin simply sighed in that way that told Jace he had hit his daily limit of understanding Zane. A never-ending challenge for the scholarly older man. But he also knew Franklin cared for the goofy comedic relief in their group.

"Skylar is the alpha in your relationship. She thinks you will always be the cheerleader to her decisions. Hence, team." Jace paused, once again stuck with the fact Zane and Skylar had a "relationship". Or that possibly, in the near future, one would exist between his two friends. Talk about a mystery. "I still can't believe you and Skylar had sex, Zane. That's more confusing than the demonic mystery we're trying to figure out." Jace smiled as he said it. "I still question which one of you has the worst taste in partners, however."

That got a pizza crust thrown by Zane and caught by Jace. Who proceeded to eat it. "My head can't wrap around it so can we table that subject for later? We need to get this Bishop issue figured out. Now, let's focus on what we know."

Franklin stood with his Yoga laptop flipped to tablet mode to review while he moved. "Amanda's going home tomorrow under hospice care. If my estimation on the character and care of her husband is correct, she won't live longer than a week, heavily sedated with morphine until she fades away. I believe Skylar had looked up their address and home type. I'll find that on the shared drive."

Jace nodded as he rubbed his jaw with his fingers and his thumb grazed over a scar. "She'll be moved by ambulance, right?" He received a nod in reply from Franklin. "And judging by the level of asshole Steven Bishop is, I am betting he'll send everyone home. No security. No care. Nothing. Just sitting and waiting for her to die." He rose to stretch next to the bed. "If not smothering her with a pillow before that."

"Okay," Zane said, "so if she's at home, she's easier to get to. But you don't need to get to her. You need to get him. So, we wait until they get to their house and 'bam, easy cheesy, lemon squeezy.' But then what? You think he's just going to confess and tell-all? 'Hey, yeah, I'm possessed by a demon and I want you dead, Camden. Oh, and here is my wife. I used her to pay off the demons.'" He leveled a sarcastic look at Jace. "I don't see that happening, dude."

It was a valid question. One Jace was unsure he had an answer for. Sure, it would be easier to get to Amanda in a residence rather than the high-dollar secured facility she had been held in. But it might not be depending on how paranoid Bishop was feeling. On the other hand, he had told them the crew was leaving. The hotel had to move them to a different room to accommodate their extended stay. And an airport shuttle left with the women. It appeared that the Dead Man's Crew had indeed, left.

"At the lake!"

Zane and Jace looked up from the devices as Franklin yelled the words. Jace frowned and Zane shrugged. "Yes, Franklin, we did the lake. You're a bit behind in the plan, old man."

Franklin countered their puzzlement with a look reflecting his own. Apparently, he thought he had said more than he had and rewound it in his head to realize he had not. "Oh, yes. No. I mean, the home of the Bishops." He turned his laptop around to show them. "They have a home on the lake. The very lake of their accident and the one that you plunged into. Further down the shore by miles nearer to Cleveland, but yet…it's at the lake."

Jace moved over to take Franklin's tablet. "That's interesting. But I'm not sure it's related at all. There's a shitload of houses on the lake." The home of the Bishops, however, was upper-scale. Not one of the simple ones he had seen in the neighborhood near the boat ramp. He zoomed in and pulled up Google maps to get a street view. "It's a gated community. That has to have a hefty price tag on it."

Jace addressed Zane as he handed Franklin the tablet back. "Didn't Sky dig for financials on the couple? The ones that were public record?"

Zane nodded. "I think so. We didn't really focus on them because of the whole demon thing. What are you thinking, Jace?"

"I'm not sure. It might be nothing." Jace sat down on the bed and picked up his laptop to log into the shared drive Skylar had set up with documents for the crew. Scrolling through the files, he picked up his phone and held it between his ear and shoulder as he called Sky. "Hey, it's me. Did we find the financial records for the Bishops' agency?"

"Aren't you even going to ask how I am?"

Jace's head jerked up when he heard Kitt's voice and angled the phone to see if he had called her number rather than Skylar's. No. "Oh hey, I uh…shit." He rubbed a hand over his face and stepped outside of the room to talk. "I didn't know you had gotten home already. I thought you were going to send me a text to let me know."

"I did. An hour ago."

Shit. Jace brought his phone down to check. The messages icon had a red three to show unread texts. One from Skylar, one from Alex, and a third from Kitt. Unnoticed and therefore, not answered. "Oh yeah, I see that now. Sorry. I just got absorbed here like an asshole." Rather than a boyfriend and the father of her child. He put his head back and slowly exhaled, carefully choosing what to say next. Words to prevent her from being hurt and crying again. "Kitt, listen."

"Here's Skylar."

There was, however, no need. She shut him down just like that. The swiftness along with the tone of finality Jace would refuse to acknowledge. In the background, he could hear Kitt's voice and Skylar's in hushed tones followed by a door slamming. He winced and dropped his chin to his chest when Skylar's voice came on the call.

"Can you tell she's pissed?"

Jace snorted at the ludicrous question. "How could I not? It's that bad, huh?

Sky sighed and her voice was edged with sympathy. "She's just hurt and it's hard to make her see your side. I think it's the preggo hormones or maybe she has that baby brain stuff going on."

Jace lifted his head to watch the cars go by on the highway. The chill in the air here creeped into his bones. Maybe recent events had scarred him on a molecular level. From being frozen just days ago. It was only fifty-degrees and midday. But it felt much colder to Jace. "Well, considering I'm not even fucking completely sure about what to do and why I'm here, it's easy to understand why she can't."

He turned to brace a hand on the closed door as he put the wind at his back. His eyes went to a dark spot on the walkway at his feet. "That's why I called. I need to figure this out fast so I can get home. Work this out with her. Focus on her and the baby. Shit, find a normal for both of them."

Skylar started laughing. "Jace, honey. You and normal are as far away from each other as Ohio is from the Gulf Coast of Texas. We're talking almost Canada distance to almost Mexico here. Do you have any idea how big of a gap there is between the two? The same can be said for Jace Camden and normal life."

"Always the consoler, Sky." He exhaled. No sense taking it out on her. It could not be easy to be both his and Kitt's friend and remain impartial. "Right. Now, the financial info. What do we have about them?"

Skylar's voice switched to a serious tone and Jace felt glad for that. He was desperate to keep his focus on why he was still in Ohio. Not on how he was not with Kitt back home in Texas. He was grateful that Skylar would have known that instinctively. They were similar in that regard. Throw yourself into work and like she said, fake it until you could make it. Jace was pretty sure that should not apply to love or relationships. He'd have to figure a different way of dealing when he got home. Apparently, what he had done during this trip was not correct.

And he was going to be a father.

That was more alien for Jace to process than Skylar and Zane hooking up.

"Jace, are you still there? Hello?"

Skylar's voice on the line snapped his mind back to the task at hand. "Yeah, sorry. Go ahead. What do you recall about their…fuck…I don't know. Their financial status? We pulled up a picture of their house and I don't know how well Ohio pays their kindergarten teachers, but they have a really nice house. Lake-shore property. Gated community with a little fancy hut for some private po-po to sit in at the entrance. I'm betting he even has air and heat. Maybe even benefits with a 401K. All of that can't be cheap."

"Right. Hold on, let me dig for a few minutes," Sky replied. Jace could hear her shuffling through belongings. They had not been home long. Most likely, her laptop was not unpacked.

Moving back inside, he set the phone down on the table. Franklin and Zane gathered around it and Jace put it on speaker when Skylar came back on the line. "Okay. So, she's an elementary teacher and he's a program management consultant. Small firm with a staff of six, according to their annual LLC report. They made less than 500K this past year in profit. That's a low income for a business in their industry and divide that among a staff, pay your overhead expenses…he's not rich. Hold on and let me see if I found anything about their home."

Jace sat in one of the chairs and tugged a cold piece of pizza from the box to chew on. He was still as cold as he had been outside. He checked the heat setting on the unit where it blew warm air under the window. Seventy-two degrees. Why the hell did he feel so cold? That question led to examining the window. He expected to see black frost creep across the glass. There was none. Only the bleak early day beyond.

Jace brought his eyes back forward to find Franklin watching him intensely and it followed with the man pressing a hand against Jace's neck. He smirked and he waved it away. The relief clear on Franklin's face to find nothing of concern. Maybe Jace had a cold—he had been dunked in a cold lake recently.

"Hmm," Skylar said it so simply. But the single syllable brought all three men to attention. It was never just a "hmm" with the sharp-minded woman. "Okay, so that house, they bought it a year ago and it's worth more than his agency makes in two years. One-million and that's hard to believe, considering. I don't see how a bank would approve such a mortgage with the income statements I'm seeing. Let me see if there's any new reports filed since the last."

Franklin and Jace met eyes at the news. Jace was still unsure how the financial details would be connected to the demons tormenting Amanda Bishop.

But something was better than nothing.

Hmm, maybe that should be his new relationship motto.

"Shit. Guys, I found their last quarterly report with the tax office. Apparently, they had a huge windfall of 1.2 million. He used that to make a half-the-price down payment on the house. No bank would turn down that high of a deposit. But where did the money come from? No idea. Only the one bump and then none. But get this…they do a press release with each new client and contract change. There were none at that time. And no new client announcements since."

Jace got to his feet and finger-combed his hair. "Skylar, there has to be something we're not seeing. Something that explains his behavior. Why does he want his wife dead?"

He chewed on his bottom lip and knew he was taking this too personally. He allowed Steven's treatment towards Amanda to be reflective on how Jace had been with Laura. Obsessed with saving her and he went to an insane level to save her soul after the suicide. He simply refused to consider that Steven Bishop did not love his wife without a valid reason. Had Kitt made the connection he had been projecting the type of man he was? Comparing himself to Steven Bishop? Had the others seen it as well?

Perhaps the members of the crew would be correct. Jace was driven by a nonexistent factor. Some husbands were just dicks and treated their wives like crap. Some men never connected to their women on a level that went deeper than a relationship status. But no, Jace knew there was something more here. There just had to be… he had risked his own relationship with Kitt to prove it. "Skylar, keep digging. Please."

She agreed to and the call ended. Jace laid back on the bed, his eyes fixated on the ceiling. He would have loved to take a nap. Dream about Kitt combing her fingers through his hair. She'd whisper words of comfort and love when he woke from a nightmare. Bathe him in a cold bath when sleep kept half of his consciousness in the realm of life, while the other half remained in the one of death. His Kitt had learned, adapted, and become the perfect companion. And here he was, fucking it up for a man like Steven Bishop.

Jace had nodded off. A tap on the shoulder from Franklin startled him awake. "Alex just sent a text. She heard from Doctor Lewis."

Jace sat up on his forearms to find Franklin's expression just as heavy as the words spoken. "Amanda is home. Bishop never set up hospice care."

CHAPTER TWENTY-ONE

"Here. Guess it's tea for you, while I drink wine for both of us the next nine-months."

Kitt sat on the deck of Jace's beach house. Funny, she had considered it "theirs" before the trip to Ohio. But now, she had no sense of home or assurance on anything. Other than the fact that Skylar's wine comment stood out stark in Kitt's reality. In less than nine months, she would have a baby. But that brought the question—would this be the baby's home too? Or just a place his or her daddy lived in when they visited?

"Thanks." Kitt lowered her head as she held the glass in her hands. Condensation already appeared on the outside of the glass in the Texas heat. Sure, it was fall, but the state didn't always acknowledge seasons. Hot, hotter, damn hot, and less hot was the normal cycle here. A source of glee for a beach girl like Kitt. Today, an odd chill penetrated the heat, which was the reason she brought the sofa throw to cocoon herself with. Who knew being pregnant meant feeling cold? Guess she needed to educate herself on being pregnant. Another nagging question arose—would she be doing that learning solo? Or with the man who made her pregnant? "Stop it," she told herself. "Just stop it." It was too upsetting to think about.

"How are they?" she asked and kept her head down. Sheesh, not that Kitt set herself up with any better with her choice of replacement topic.

"Don't you mean to really ask how *he* is?"

Kitt did a soft snort. "Yeah. Guess you know me way too well, huh?" She rested her head sideways on the back of the worn Adirondack chair. She gave Skylar a slight smile as she sat in the one next to Kitt. "So are you going to tell me how Jace is or do I have to be more conniving to get the info out of you?"

Skylar laughed and drew her knees up against her chest. "They are trying, but not finding much new. Jace had me dig into the Bishops' financials. Nothing revealing there. I'm not sure what bank reports and tax reports have to do with supernatural activity. But hey, I don't have his job."

Kitt let out a snarky laugh. She knew Skylar was not referencing the founder of a non-profit consulting agency position. The Camden Agency ran itself. And it paid its founder very well. With the exception of Jace having to sign-off on contracts or large grant documents, they almost never needed him to come into the office. Kitt had thought the benefit of that would be that he'd be here with her more. Not traveling all over the country. Like Ohio. Where he *chose* to fight demons other than his own.

"Job. Is that what we're calling it now? I have to say, if we're going to do that, it needs to pay far better than it does now. As it is, the benefits suck."

Kitt brought a hand up to wipe over her eyes. "I hate it, Sky. And I know he was like this before I met him. And I know if I really love him, I should not want to change him. I don't. I just want to change how we deal with it."

She let out a deep sigh and tried to focus on the surf as it gently washed over the sand. "I know a normal relationship is impossible with Jace. But I'm pregnant. He should be home. Not there. Fighting to save a woman he doesn't even know. He needs to be here." Her hand moved to her stomach. "With us."

Skylar reached out to take Kitt's hand in hers. "I know. But Kitt, this is how Jace is. I think part of him will always regret that the demon that tortured him and Laura for so long got away. That he couldn't kill the bitch for what she had done. He will never admit it. But he was denied vengeance." Skylar met Kitt's eyes as she spoke. It was easy to see the conviction Skylar showed in the words she spoke to validate Jace's behavior.

Kitt, on the other hand, was not so sure. "I don't know, Skylar. I thought I did. I thought I knew him."

"Kitt, I think he's trying to not be eaten up by it. Maybe, by ending the demon or demons torturing Amanda Bishop, he will feel he has rid himself of the guilt of failing Laura." Skylar pursed her lips together and sat back in her chair. "Or I could be completely wrong, and the courts were right all along. Your boyfriend is bat shit crazy." But the smile was fake—it didn't even reach her eyes.

Kitt tugged the throw tighter around her. "Maybe." She did not dare say what followed that word. When would he start feeling guilt for failing her?

"Can I tell you something?" She found a loose piece of yarn on the throw to twist in her fingers. "I planned on doing something before all this Ohio stuff came up." She closed her eyes and her head hit the back of the chair with a thud. "I was going to propose to him. To Jace. I was going to ask *him* to marry *me*." She laughed. Skylar jerked to sit upright and turned in her chair. "I know. He hates marriage. The thought of it. And I know why. He's scared. But maybe with the baby coming…"

"Kitt! Did you get knocked up on purpose?" Skylar bolted out of seat to squat in front of Kitt's and took her hand in a tight grip. "Kitt! Did you?"

"No! Of course not! Sheesh!" She jerked her hand away and glared at her friend. "Are you kidding me? How could you think that? It was just as much of a surprise to me! I didn't even know I was until the day we left for Ohio. I bought the pregnancy test when we were getting supplies at the store that morning. I went to pack tampons the night before and realized I was more than a month late with my period."

Kitt stood, taking the throw with her before she leaned against the deck rail. The waves beyond were her usual coping mechanism when her emotions overwhelmed her but provided zero comfort now. "That led to me needing to tell him. Then the fleeting idea of proposing. Afterall, aren't all of you always telling me how unique a relationship me and Jace have?" She glanced back at Sky. "Why should who proposed to whom be any different?"

Skylar joined her at the rail. "Wow. I don't know Kitt." She looked over at her. "Here I was thinking Jace was the crazy one in your relationship." Kitt knew her friend joked when she received a shoulder bump. "But how is he going to take that? Are you just setting yourself up to be upset again?" Skylar pivoted to rest her hip on the rail. "Don't take this wrong, but you've been acting really strange this past week. Harder on Jace than I've ever seen you be. And leaving? Kitt, that's not you."

Skylar looked down as she spoke as if she didn't want Kitt to see how much she hated stating the truth. It hadn't been like her. No wonder Jace and the rest were confused.

Kitt thought about it and turned to sit against the railing. The warmth of the deck wood under her barely penetrating through that chill. Skylar moved to sit next to her in silence to await a response. "I don't know, Sky. I wish I did. Maybe it's the pregnancy? The hormones or maybe both triggered some bitch switch I didn't know I have."

She leaned to the side to rest her head on Skylar's shoulder. "I just needed to go. I can't bear to see him taking another chance. But I don't even know where that intolerance comes from. When he's taken these chances before, I wanted to be right there. Even when he didn't want me to be. But now," she closed her eyes and her voice cracked, "I wanted to be as far away as I could get."

They sat in silence. Kitt was glad Skylar chose to break through it. Kitt didn't know how. "From him? You wanted to get far away from him? Or the situation? The danger?"

The only response Kitt could give confused her even more. "That's the thing, Sky. I don't know."

CHAPTER TWENTY-TWO

"Are we sure this isn't just going to get you killed for real this time?"

Jace buttoned up his dress shirt as Zane fidgeted nearby. Glancing over to answer, he shrugged. "I have no idea. But if pushing Bishop's buttons to get more information from him doesn't work, I am not sure how to proceed."

After Skylar could not get any more details, the three of them discussed next possible steps. Jace was running out of ideas. Amanda Bishop was a sedated, dying captive in a home shared with Steven Bishop. A man Jace believed wanted her dead with no ironclad reason why.

He placed a small Bluetooth device in his ear. It was set up to record live from his phone to Zane's tablet. He and Franklin would listen as they waited in the rental near the Bishop residence while Jace confronted Steven.

"Testing…one, two, three." Jace twisted at the waist to hear his voice come through the tablet speaker as it recorded. "Great. This thing has a range of a thousand feet, so we should be fine."

Franklin tested the link a second time, ever over-cautious. Zane rolled his eyes at the doubt in his geekhood. It did nothing to elevate Franklin's worried expression. "I'll be ready to dial 911 if he becomes violent and hostile. I do not believe he will be thrilled you stopped by for a visit."

Jace smirked in agreement. "Let's just fucking hope I'm right and he gets a case of 'stupid under stress.' I bet he's like every other bully I've crossed in my life. An 'all bark and no bite' kind of guy." Jace rolled his head on his neck to shrug the persistent chill and met his reflection in the mirror in front of him. "It would not help my efforts with Kitt or worth the heartache I've put her through if we fail. And if I *do* go home a failure, I'd like to not be limping with a broken limb or two. It would make for one painful flight home." He blew out some tension, but it was a waste of breath—literally. Jace needed Bishop to slip up. A confession. Something. "Are we ready to go and get this done?"

Zane stood with gear stowed in his worn messenger bag. "Go Team Jace!" He held his fist out for a tap. Jace smirked and he walked past without accepting the "bro" gesture. Franklin did even less by not acknowledging him at all. Zane mumbled as they exited the room, "I don't think you guys know what the word 'team' means."

"No car in the drive," Zane said from the backseat. The rental car was parked down the street from the Bishop home. They had been lucky to tailgate behind a takeout delivery person who possessed the gate code. Otherwise, Jace had planned on walking from the community entrance. Jace would pray luck gifted them more tonight.

The sky was dark, clouds covering the moon, and a cold wind blew off of Lake Erie. The sight of the waves on the frigid silver water stirred his nauseating anxiety. It made Jace long for the Texas heat back home.

"Doesn't mean he's not home. There's a two-car garage. And the lights are on in the back part of the house. Saw that when we came around the corner." The Bishop home, like many homes at the lake's edge, was constructed with windows to admire the view. Jace noticed there were no curtains or they were drawn back. Either would allow him to see into the home within and maybe before being spotted. A slim advantage, but Jace would take it. "I'm going to see if I can get a look at how Amanda is doing."

He quietly exited the car and closed the door carefully behind him. He jogged up the slope of the side yard and entered a privacy fence enclosed in the back through an unlocked gate. The tall fence ran along the two sides with the back edge of the property open to the lake beyond. The area near the shore was littered with lounging chairs and a table, complete with an ice chest built in. Jace had one similar back home at the beach house for beers and ice.

Just the reminder of his deck furniture had Jace longing for home. And for Kitt.

He reached the back patio and stayed low in the shadows. He found himself able to view the interior of the house through floor-to-ceiling windows into the living room, or it had been before Amanda had been brought home to die. A leather sofa and matching love-seat had been shoved to the side to make for a hospital bed in the center of the space. A fire crackled in the cavernous fireplace. A huge wall-mounted, flat-screen television was turned on across from her. As if the woman could watch whatever played. Jace wanted to know if being home had improved the woman's condition. The drool dripping from her chin and the lax composure of her face verified it had not. An IV pole sat to the right of Amanda's head. Jace noticed that the tubing with its puncturing needle was looped over the unplugged IV pump. For a split-second,

Jace feared they were too late and Amanda had already expired. But no, her chest made that butterfly chest motion. She had not died.

Yet.

Without the morphine, did the woman suffer in pain? Did it matter to her husband? Sure, Jace's confidence level that Bishop wanted Amanda to die could not be higher. But the fact he would keep the morphine drip from his wife to ease her last moments pissed Jace off. The rage of it burnt the chill of the lake wind. Jace could not stand cruelty and what he had witnessed of the Bishops was beyond cruel. It bordered on psychotic. Jace might be crazy, but never close to the level of depravity of Steven Bishop towards his wife.

As if summoned by Jace's ill thoughts, Steven appeared into the view. He walked over to stand next to Amanda's bed. Jace moved around the outdoor living space for a better line of sight. He thought at first, the man would bend over to give his dying wife a kiss.

But Jace was wrong. So fucking wrong.

Steven Bishop moved to crawl up the hospital bed on his hands and knees. He appeared to be sniffing her scent like a dog would when discovering a dead animal in a field. To roll on its decomposing body. To cover itself in the scent of death.

Horrifyingly fixated, Jace moved closer to the window for a better view to attempt to understand what he was witnessing. Bishop continued to crawl until he was parallel with his wife's face. His weight held up on bent arms while he continued the sniffing action.

"What the fuck?" Jace whispered and jerked back as a black, wispy form emerged from Bishop like a shadow, but nothing as jovially delightful as the one that kept escaping Peter Pan. This one was more tangible. Phantasm, yet whole. Bishop twitched oddly as the form mimicked the actions of prowling over his wife's body. Jace realized it was very similar to the inky forms in the glass cube.

"Demon," Jace snarled as he stepped closer to the glass. This demon inhaled Amanda's breath and Jace could see a strange sparking between them. Her back arched off the bed. A silent scream twisted her face. The demon pulled what Jace guessed was Amanda's soul from her fragile body. Its energy so weak, it barely glowed.

"Hey!" Jace slammed his fists against the glass with a resounding thud. "Hey! Fucker! Get away from her!" Both Steven and the demon whipped their heads to the side to regard him. Jace could see the glowing ice-blue eyes of the demon over Steven's unfocused blank face. "Yeah, that's right you ugly fucker. I can see you. Surprise!"

At first, the demon seemed confused at being seen. Its head lifted up to hear something Jace could not. It then turned back towards him and Jace could have sworn the bastard smiled. Actually, frightening as fuck, it smiled.

"Shit."

Jace had not considered what to do beyond distracting the thing. Taunting it was most likely also unwise. He just wanted to stop it from devouring what was left of Amanda's weak soul. Did Jace give thought to the cause and effect of his actions? No.

Maybe he needed to build that skill if he survived.

Now was not the time as Steven leaped off of Amanda's body. Jace was able to see the demon wrapped around its host like a shroud. It animated the man's limbs like a monstrous puppet master. Steven moved with floor-eating strides, but his face still showed no reaction. He reached the French doors and stepped onto the patio.

Jace strode backwards and tensed for a fight as the demon-possessed man turned to face him. He picked up a patio chair and ran down a summary of what was happening to Zane and Franklin via the device in his ear. "He was about to kill her. I distracted him by showing him I was here. And now, I think I'm about to get my ass kicked by him and the demon jerking his asshole strings."

Franklin and Zane both told him to run. To get back to the car. Jace knew that would target his friends. The demons used who Jace cared in the past either for distraction or a desperate ploy to prevent being ended. It had succeeded before. The demon tormenting Laura had escaped.

Jace would not let that happen again. "Nah, I got this. This bastard isn't getting away."

The demon rushed towards him. Jace met it with the heavy patio chair swung into its side. The damn thing barely flinched. Jace tossed the bent chair to the side and the demon laughed at him.

"Great, this is going to suck." Jace raised his arms up in a defensive blocking pose. The demon evidently did not abide by the rules of boxing as it lifted Jace up in a bear hug with supernatural strength. A level impossible for Steven or any human to possess.

Jace succeeded to pull one arm free from the embrace to bring an elbow blow to the demon's shoulder. The death hug loosened enough for Jace to be able to at least breathe. He tugged his other arm out and let out a yell as the demon began to squeeze. Jace continued to struggle even as he lost the ability to breathe.

"Us know you. *Cammmdeeen.*" the demon cackled in bizarre glee, Steven's voice distorted from its manipulation. Jace barely understood the words and wished he hadn't. The possession or whatever the fuck it was made the demon's cloak thick. Jace only caught a glimpse of the human man beneath it. Jace could clearly see the demon's glowing ice-toned eyes and long fangs. Jagged and faceted like icicles. "Us brought you here. It was easy. We called. And you came." It laughed a nightmare-inducing sound. Its head moved close to hiss in Jace's ear. A frozen, slick tongue flicked over his neck. "You came here to die."

The demon began to run and Jace realized its goal was the dark lake. The shore rushed up fast and he struggled to suck in a gulp of air as they reached the water's edge. The demon then fell forward with more laughter. Jace was the one to land under the surface of the frigid water on his back, the cold mud strangely soft under him. A watery, comfy bed for Jace to drown in—for the third time in a week.

He struggled, arms flailing out of the water to claw at the demon and Steven. His lungs gulped for air when they emptied of it. And replaced the void with water. He grew weaker and he could hear his heart beating too fast. Too loud.

His mind grasped onto something to rally him to survive and the imagery of Kitt holding out the pregnancy test was the first to arise. If he died here, he would never be able to tell her how excited he was. How the fear that she carried his child had gotten in the way of the larger joy. How he wanted to paint the nursery yellow. And he knew she would hate that. But he'd change her mind. Convince her with kisses and laughter to do it anyway.

Fuck, he was never going to meet his baby.

Franklin shrieked into his cell phone as a 911 operator grilled him. Zane and he were out of the car. They ran up the slope that led to the gate of the backyard of the Bishop residence. The woman on the dispatch call asked him the nature of his emergency. He couldn't reply that he believed Jace's face might be getting eaten by a demon. Franklin lied to say he witnessed a burglar breaking into the home. The operator said that police were on the way and to stay on the line until help arrived. Franklin hung up the call and prayed they hurried.

"It's stuck!"

Franklin caught up to Zane and had expected the younger, faster man to have already reached where they believed Jace to be. The audio link had gone to static a few seconds after they heard him hit the lake. "What?"

He grasped the gate latch and yelped to find it ice cold. He lifted his hand and his eyes went wide as he saw black frost melting off his hand. The latch was frozen and coated in it. "Zane! We have got to get in there!"

Zane reached out to move him back, brought up a foot, and kicked the gate. It didn't budge. Zane yelled and struck the wooden gate again. Franklin rounded the corner to find another way in. The fence was over seven-feet high with a line of wire. He guessed it served a dual purpose of being both stylish and electrified. He saw the lake beyond and yelled to Zane. Both took off running to the end of the fence where it opened onto the water.

"I honestly don't think there's anything left to watch that I haven't seen, Sky." She put a hand on her stomach and whispered downward to the tiny person within. "You were probably conceived during a 'Netflix and chill' moment, little baby."

Kitt was in the kitchen pouring herself some tea and grabbed a beer for Skylar when a strange pain hit. The glass in her hand crashed to the floor and shattered on the tile at her feet. She let out a gasp and bent at the waist as both hands spread protectively over her stomach.

Sky, of course, hearing the breaking glass, ran in with alarm on her face. "What happened?" Her eyes went to Kitt's belly as she paled. "Oh my god! Kitt!"

Kitt tried to suck in a breath, a difficult task as the pain grew sharp and sudden. "I don't know. Oh god, Sky, I don't know."

Suddenly, Jace was jerked up from the water. The demon straddled him with his shirt held in its fists. Jace gasped and sputtered up water as he brought his hands up to wrap around the demon's wrist. It came in low with an odd expression on its face. "A baby?"

Jace's eyes widened at those two otherwise simple words. He realized the demon must have heard Jace's desperate thoughts. He snarled as he brought a fist up to hit the demon hard in the side of the head. Now his own strength became inhuman. Call it dormant soul warrior skills or that of a father fueled by the need to protect his child. Jace had no idea.

The force behind his punch caused the demon to list to the side and release its hold. Jace sputtered as he stumbled to his feet and stalked after it. It tried to stand and he straight-kicked it so hard, it lifted off the ground.

When the demon crashed in a heap to the grass, the strange dark cloaking flickered. Perhaps its ability to attach to Steven Bishop had been damaged. Maybe Bishop took the blows. Didn't make any difference to Jace's onslaught. He dropped to his knees to straddle the demon and the man it was losing control of. He struck again and again. His fist wailed on the demon and the face of Steven Bishop. He yelled in anger with each blow. Blood slicked his knuckles. They split from the force of his hits to the sharpened fangs of the demon and the human mass beneath it. The demon made an effort to fight back, but neither Jace's mind nor body registered any damage or pain it inflicted.

Jace reared his fist back again but his downward arch halted. The demon began to separate from Steven. The process tore the dark, thick, oozing fibers and the pulsing remains clumsily scurried towards the lake before it fully detached.

Maybe Jace would find it amusing later that demons, no matter the form they took, were all fucking cowards in the end.

The one that had possessed his wife had run to save its ass from being destroyed and this one tried to escape as well. But the last time, Jace had been dead on a table. This time, he was very much alive. And he was fucking pissed.

Jace got to unsteady feet. His body threatened to go to one knee a few times as he stalked after the demon. His body needed him to stop. His heart begged with beats like a drum going off in his skull. But Jace would not let another demon escape. Not again.

He caught it in the shallows of the lake. He wrapped his hands around its oozing, disgusting form. Like grabbing a live eel covered in oil. It reminded Jace of the tar balls that washed up on the sands of Galveston island whenever one of the oil rigs off the coast had a spill. The demon looked as surprised as Jace that he could hold it. He couldn't blame it for that lack of knowledge. Jace didn't know he could either. He brought it up with his legs braced far apart, feet sunk deep in the mud of the freezing lake and wrapped his hands around its bulb-shaped head.

It screamed and squealed as Jace went close to its ghoulish face and snarled a threat for it to take with it. "Go to fucking hell. And when you get there? Tell the bitch demon that got away if she or any of your kind go near my baby, I will come after you. And I will end you all."

Jace squeezed and the demon exploded. Its ooze splattering Jace as his legs gave way. Tendrils and pieces of it hit the water, drifting down like torn paper. A greasy, busted balloon. It sank out of sight below the surface. But he knew, just fucking knew as he crashed to his knees it was dead. There would be no more demons getting away.

"Freeze! Get your hands behind your head! Now!"

Glancing weakly back over his shoulder, a pressed hand on his chest over his heart. The organ felt like it would explode like the demon had. Steven Bishop struggled to sit up, the man's face no longer blank. No, it held an alarming volume of bewilderment. Behind him, two police officers had entered the yard through the gate. One advanced towards Steven and the other towards Jace. The gate swung open and he got a glimpse of Franklin and Zane on their knees in the yard. The property was lit up in a red and blue way all too familiar to Jace.

This must have been Bishop's first time being arrested. The man was having a mental breakdown. He ranted in a crazed babble that demons made him do it. Jace snorted with a cough, "Good luck convincing them of that, asshole." The cop repeated the order about the hands again and Jace obeyed as they went behind his head. He did his best not to fall face-first in the mud.

As the officer reached him, Jace pointed to the house before the cuffs were snapped on his wrists. "There is a woman. In the house. She needs help. Please." He was jerked to his feet and he closed his eyes in relief as the officer called for an ambulance. More cops arrived at the scene and Jace was placed in the backseat of one of the patrol units. Sagging against the back seat as it pulled away, he watched an ambulance pull up to the residence. Jace had no idea if help had arrived in time.

CHAPTER TWENTY-THREE

"Camden, wake up. You've been released."

He had been placed in the county holding cell since last night. For the first few hours, he kept himself from freaking out by watching the second hand run around the caged clock high up on the concrete wall. Exhaustion had given him reprieve as well. He was pretty sure getting the shit beat out of him had also assisted. With drawn up knees, Jace rested his forehead on them to doze a few blessed minutes of actual sleep. Those, however, had been few and far between. He was dizzy, ached all over, and was extremely grumpy.

Jace had zero idea what would happen yet. Afterall, he did have a criminal background of previous assaults. Not to mention, he had been put on trial for murder. Imagining how badly it could go had his anxiety banging around his head like an angry wasp in a jar, the lid twisted tight, the air running out.

"Me?"

The officer nodded. Jace stood and groaned as his legs, his back, and the rest of him protested. He hurt from hair to his still-soaked shoes. He sported dozens of cuts both shallow and deep and dark bruises from battling a demon the night before. He was shown out and the cell locked behind him. The officer had to catch him once on the way down the hall as Jace combed his fingers through his hair and plucked a twig out of it. And almost fell down.

"Are you sure it's me you're supposed to release?"

They had reached another locked door. It buzzed and the officer responded with a shrug. "Charges were dropped. Make sure the desk sergeant has your contact info in case they need more information." He handed Jace a manila envelope of his personal belongings as Jace stepped into the room beyond. "How? Why?"

Jace stared at the man in dazed confusion. He did more of the same at the door as it closed behind him. No way could it be this easy. "What? Why?"

"He confessed. Bishop. To everything." He turned at the voice behind him and found Skylar there. She threw her arms around his shoulders to hug. She squeezed until he let out a grunt of pain. She backed up enough to get a get a look at him. "You look like shit. Jail is not a good look on you, dead guy."

Jace's eyes moved beyond to the discharge waiting area. Sky pressed a hand against his cheek to bring his focus back. "Zane and Franklin were released hours ago and are at the hotel. We have a flight leaving as soon as I can make the arrangements." She wound her arm around his waist and led him to the exit and the sunny winter day outside. "Wait here. I'll go get the car. You look like you're ready to fall over."

Jace very willingly did as he was told and dropped to sit on a metal bench in front of the courthouse building. He let his head fall forward and closed his eyes. It was taking some serious effort to not actually fall over. Concrete had never looked so good as a place to take a nap.

"Mr. Camden."

He heard a soft, strange voice say his name. When he lifted his eyes, he found a frail, thin woman sitting in a wheelchair in front of him. Jace frowned as he tried to recognize her through the haze in his mind. It wasn't until she tugged her sweater sleeve down that he caught a glimpse of healing cuts resembling the letters "D.E.N."

"Amanda." Recognition sizzled his mind to wide open and awake. "I mean…Mrs. Bishop."

She gave him a soft smile. "Yes. They told me inside you were released. I'm glad I was able to see you before you left." Her voice was weak. The energy it took to just have a conversation appeared very draining. But she was alive, her eyes intense and focused. Much better than the last time Jace had seen her. "I know we didn't really ever meet. But I feel like we know each other." She gave a slight laugh and brushed a lock of her hair behind her ear. "It's strange, I know. But they said you helped stop Steven."

Her thin face lowered as she fidgeted with a throw on her lap. "I can't thank you enough. Even if I don't quite understand how you did it." She lifted her eyes back to his. "Or why." Amanda's pale hand reached out to take Jace's in hers. It was comforting and warm. "But thank you."

He frowned and opened his mouth to explain, but perhaps it was better if he didn't. She would be led to believe whatever reason Bishop gave for his actions. Jace wasn't sure if Amanda's husband *knew that* demons had pulled his strings. Most likely not. Olivia, Laura's sister, did not realize demons had whispered in her ear. Told her to make Jace fail. To push him closer and closer to committing suicide.

As Jace took in the kindness in Amanda's eyes and her gentle nature, he told himself she had been through enough. The both of them had. "You're welcome."

Jace looked up when a car pulled up. Skylar exited it and he rose to his feet. "Good luck. It's good to see you recovering, Mrs. Bishop." Their eyes locked and there was something there in her gaze.

Jace thought that perhaps, she recalled more than he wished she had. But like any nightmare, the longer the sleeper was awake, the less the nightmare could be remembered. "Take care."

Jace stepped past to meet Skylar halfway when Amanda grabbed his hand. For a moment, she looked panicked and afraid. She jerked him down and Jace's stomach churned. His head pounded as he met her eyes. He suddenly, without explanation, wanted to escape. The hairs on the back of his neck rose and it felt as if that thick liquid of the cube surrounded them once more. She lifted her head to press her mouth against his ear and said, "There's evil in your world, Mr. Camden. And no soul is too small."

And then she let him go. The warning sensations vanished and she gave him a smile. Jace wondered if he had imagined it. But no, the tickle of a nose bleed in his sinuses told him differently. "You take care too, Mr. Camden. Goodbye."

As Amanda Bishop was wheeled into the police station, Jace closed his eyes. He was so fucking tired. That freaky little scene must have been a manifestation of exhaustion. When Skylar reached him, he dropped his head forward to meet her eyes with a weary smile. "How about we leave tomorrow and I sleep until the flight leaves. You can wheel me to the gate on one of those baggage cart things."

Skylar took his hand and Jace's humor fled. She had a strange expression on her face.

"What happened?"

"It's Kitt and the baby." She bit her bottom lip nervously. "She was rushed to the hospital last night. We can't wait for a later flight."

Jace Camden was a mess—physically, emotionally, and mentally a wreck. It had zero to do with being on an airplane. Skylar had gotten them all on a redeye flight from Ohio to Houston, Texas. And the more Skylar tried to reassure him that Kitt and his baby were fine, the less he believed it. He wanted to hold Kitt. Hear the details from the doctors. He wanted to see the mother of his child. Somehow *know* their baby was unharmed. Kitt had the pain at the same time as the fight. The demon that knew about the baby, Jace had killed. But why did that not offer him a little comfort?

Skylar used the information about the Bishops to distract him from her seat next to him. Steven Bishop had been working covertly for a very large pharmaceutical company. Steven had been paid under the table by the company responsible for flooding the state of Ohio with opioids. The company had record profits they needed to hide. Watchdog agencies sniffed around to call foul as the epidemic grew to be a hot topic in the media, which caught the attention of a legislative anti-big pharm lobbyist. Steven confessed to being paid to cover profit reports. To funnel the money through his agency and in turn, he was paid a million dollars for the deed.

If Jace and the others had looked deeper into the Bishop Agency's LLC reports, they would have found the primary chief owner on paper was Amanda Bishop. The agency was funded with money from her father's life insurance when he had passed seven years ago.

According to Amanda's police statement, the day of the wreck, she had discovered the second set of financial records. She had the sweet idea of surprising her husband by finally unpacking his office in their house. They had plans to go out to dinner that night. Amanda confronted her husband on the way to the restaurant and an argument ensued. She would shut the agency down. It was the smartest thing to do before the law and the government became aware of the scheme.

She hated to be associated with a company responsible for thousands of people dying weekly due to opioid addictions. Steven hadn't been receptive. They needed the money. Didn't she understand who had paid for that fancy new house? Amanda had not cared. Neither the money, nor the house meant anything to her. And it shouldn't be what was important to him.

She had no memory of the wreck from the moment the car went off the road. But Steven Bishop had filled in the rest with his statement.

Steven Bishop had wanted to go in and rescue Amanda from the vehicle, but something had stopped him. He told the detective who took his confession, "I swear, I told myself to let her die. But it couldn't be me. I love my wife. But I stopped and I did nothing." Steven had broken down and admitted to everything.

Skylar read aloud the reports in a hushed tone to avoid waking the sleeping passengers overhearing her. Jace turned his head to look out the plane's window at the night sky beyond. While his eyes took in the view, his mind was disengaged from admiring as it processed the recent events.

Steven had wanted to go into the car and save his wife, but "something" had stopped him. Jace knew without a single doubt that had been the moment the demons attached to Steven Bishop. The demons were drawn to Amanda's soul as it flickered between life and death. A way to the land of the living. To use an innocent person as a pawn to get another chance at killing him. The demon at the lake had all but said that very thing. As much as Jace didn't want to consider it, he had no choice.

There were millions of humans living on the planet. He turned his head back towards Skylar and his eyes went to the amulet on her wrist. He thought by isolating those he cared for, he alone would be a target of the demons. He was so tragically wrong.

There weren't enough amulets to be made for every single person in the world. Some would die or come close to it every single second. On every single day. The catastrophic possibilities made Jace want to jump out of the plane and die. If he actually could.

Could he die? Or had he just been fortunate enough to be brought back? Laura had not believed so. Jace began to fear she was right. It was not a gift. More like a curse.

"What are you thinking, Jace? Did you hear anything I just said?"

His eyes lifted to Skylar's. He halted the path his mind dared to venture down. It was too overwhelming. Jace needed to focus on getting home. To see Kitt and cocoon her, their baby, and the whole crew in some way. Jace had zero idea how. There had to be a way to turn the tides in the realms only he could step into.

But not today. Not tonight. Maybe tomorrow.

"Nah. I'm just exhausted. Ready to get home. That's all." He leaned to her and planted a soft kiss on his friend's forehead. As he slumped down in the seat, he crossed his arms around himself and closed his eyes. He vaguely felt Skylar wrap one of the airline blankets around him and place a soft kiss on his cheek. And Jace finally got a hard-won nap.

CHAPTER TWENTY-FOUR

"Mom, no. I don't need you to come here." Kitt laid her head back against the hospital bed with one hand holding her cell against her ear and the other splayed protectively over her stomach. Her eyes wandered to the monitors. Although she was told it was too soon to hear the baby's heartbeat, she wished she could have seen that rather than hers on the display. "Uh, they said it was some digestive issues."

Alex, who sat in a chair in the corner, raised a brow in amusement at Kitt's cover. She did not want to tell her parents she was pregnant over the phone. Her mother and father had moved to Florida when she had moved into Jace's place. Her mother adored the man. Her father…well, no one would ever be good enough for his "little girl". Even if Kitt was almost thirty-years old. "Yeah, they just wanted to milk the insurance, I think, by keeping me overnight. Do not come here. I bet you guys haven't even unpacked."

When her mother asked how Jace was handling it, Kitt winced. She lied and said fine. She honestly had no idea. When Franklin had called Skylar, she had left to go back to Ohio. Kitt was assured that Jace was fine. She would have to trust her friend to make sure of it. She had hoped to get a call from him. A text. Something. Maybe Jace was no surer than Kitt of where they stood in the relationship. She bit her bottom lip as the call ended with her mother, luckily, more at ease and no longer threatening to come back to Texas. Kit lowered her cell to the bed and let out a long sigh. She was ready to go home and fidgeted at a loose thread on a rip at the knee of her jeans to waste time.

When the door opened, she thought it was the nurse finally bringing her discharge paperwork. Kitt lifted her head and put on her most grateful smile. She dropped it to see it was not a medical person, but it was Jace.

He looked beaten. A black eye on one side of his face and cuts with bruises on the opposite cheek and brow. Exhaustion drawn on his face. Steps slow and his stance slumped. But when his eyes met hers, they were full of worry and apology.

Kitt had practiced several times how to rip him a new one when he got there. Those plans vaporized and she was off the bed to rush into his arms to hug. The force of her embrace had his back hitting the wall behind him as his arms went around her.

Kitt sobbed as she lifted back enough to plant kisses all over his face, lips grazing over every boo-boo she could see. "Oh god. Look at you. You look awful." She said the words with a huge smile on her face and tears ran down her cheeks. Her hand then swung to smack him hard on the chest. "And what took you so long!?"

Jace would have laughed if not for his concern for Kitt and their baby. He moved her to the bed and gently pushed her to sit. He went to one knee on the floor in front of her. Not the best idea since he was not sure he'd be able to get up, but he was already there now. He pressed his face against her stomach, wrapped his arms around her and breathed in her scent. Sand, sun, and Kitt. With a touch of Doritos. He let out a small laugh about that piece of intel.

He lifted his head as he said softly, "I was in jail. If you must know. And I couldn't call you because my phone got ruined in a lake. While I was fighting a demon." He smiled as her eyes widened with each bit of information. "Which I was able to kill. Which was pretty fucking cool while being equally just as disgusting as you might imagine." He smirked. "And I drowned. A third time. In the span of a week." He moved enough to put a hand on her belly. "How are you and the baby?"

Kitt cupped his face and sank down to his eye level. "You know you're going to have to expand and explain aaaalll of that, right, mister?"

Jace nodded. "And I will. But first you. Baby. Condition. What happened?"

Kitt nodded as he joined her on the bed. Alex came over to give him a careful hug and gave them the excuse that she needed more coffee so she could leave the two of them alone. Jace took Kitt's hand in his and turned to take a more intense look at her. Her eyes were clear, the bridge of her nose sprinkled with its delightful freckles he adored and as lame as he found the term in the past, she glowed. "Now, Skylar said the doctors said it was fluke? Nothing is wrong?"

Kitt rested her head on his shoulder, wrapped an arm around him to be as close as possible, and nodded. "I had this pain. It was so sudden and sharp. It scared me more than anything, but then once I got here, I was fine." Jace felt the way her face lifted against his arm that she was smiling. "But it's official now by not only the pee stick, but by the doctors and a blood test." She lifted her eyes to his. "We're pregnant. They think I'm around six weeks." She had tears of an acceptable type now in the blue depths of her eyes. Jace brought his fingers up to wipe them away as she laughed. "We need to set up an appointment in a few weeks for the first ultrasound, but it will be too soon to find out if it's a boy or girl and…"

She wasn't able to finish her sentence. Jace brought his mouth to hers without warning and claimed it in a sizzling, emotional kiss. The whole drive from the airport to the hospital, including the ferry across Galveston Bay, he had thought of how he handled the news of Kitt telling him she was pregnant the first time. How he had screwed up the moment. How one day, if their child ever asked how Daddy behaved when Mommy told him she was pregnant, they would have to either outright lie or be crafty with their answer.

A kiss such as the one he gave Kitt in that moment should have been how he handled it. A kiss that he hoped not only intertwined with her heart, but wrapped around the tiny baby growing in the haven in her belly. To let him or her know they are loved. A kiss that spoke of all the love, faith, hope, and devotion he felt for the woman who was gifting him with a baby. A blessing he never thought heaven, fate, destiny, or karma would find him worthy of.

A kiss.

Just like this.

"Oh, sorry."

Jace lifted his mouth from Kitt's, both of them breathless from it. He chuckled with his head resting on her shoulder and she spoke to the nurse. The woman had brought Kitt's discharge papers and then left. He sat up and lifted the papers from the end of the bed. He noted the appointment set for a gynecologist in two weeks. "It says you have to rest." He brought his eyes to meet hers. "Rest. Says it right here in black and white."

Kitt moved off the bed with an eye roll. "Oh no, Mr. Camden, you are not going to be one of those boyfriends." She slung her big, worn messenger bag over her shoulder. Or she tried to right before Jace jerked it away from her. "Do not be like that. I am not some weak woman who needs you to coddle her."

She put her hands on her hips, a cute brow went up and she gave him a dead-serious look. "I mean it. Rest does not mean bedrest. Rest means I go home and you rub my feet and pet my hair but let me do what I want when I get bored with all of that." She bent at the waist with a wide smile, a crinkled nose, and put a hand on his chest. "I am not the old one with a bad heart, now am I?" She stabbed her finger harder against him. "Who then goes out and beats up demons and fights people who have demons, now am I?"

She realized what she so flippantly stated and tears sprung to her eyes. "Oh god, Jace, you, you…" She sniffed and sobbed hard in amazingly quick time to Jace. "You could have died! Baby, you have a bad heart! Our baby could have been born without a father…"

And—he kissed her again to halt her from saying more. With as much passion and determination as before, but completely with different motives. Before had been to correct a wrong. This one was to correct what she thought would go wrong. Related. Yet. Not.

When her hands rested on his chest and a sigh mixed with the kiss, he lifted his head to smile against her lips. "I would say don't call me old, but after giving you that, you might want to do it all the time."

She smiled as her arms came up to wrap around his neck. "You would be right." She gave him a mock pout. "How about you just give me kisses like that just because. If you ever stop, I'll just start to cry again." She paused and narrowed her eyes. "Wait a minute…did you just do that to *stop* me from crying?"

Jace shrugged and pressed his lips together and turned his eyes upward. "Nah." But the wink that followed gave him away. But she didn't seem to mind…

Because he kissed her again.

CHAPTER TWENTY-FIVE

It had been two weeks since Jace had returned from Ohio. He and Kitt had spent the time locked away in their home. They got lost in each other. Cleaned out the spare room in the beach house. He had indeed told her he wanted to paint it yellow—it was suitable for either gender. She, as he predicted, shot that color down and wanted a green. And just as he also believed, he changed her mind with kisses and convenient back rubs as he discussed how soothing the color would be.

The room was now half-painted yellow with splatters of it on the floor. He and Kitt had played with the rollers and ended up making love on the drop sheets. They had splotches of paint on their skin and splatters of it in their hair. They laid on the floor with his shirt bunched under her head to use for a pillow as she curled up next to him.

"I think we should move."

It came out of his mouth before his brain could give it much thought. Kitt rose up to rest on her elbow to look down at him in confusion. "See, you decided on yellow for the baby's room and you hate it so much you want to move. I told you it was ugly."

Jace sat upright, braced on his hands and looked around the room. "No, it's nice. But that's not it." He twisted to face her and sat cross-legged. He frowned for a moment as he organized his thoughts. "I think I might be sick of water after drowning three times. I once loved it here. Being by the beach, but then this house. I was running from my past when I found it." He looked around. "The demon bitch attacked you here. Her ghost haunted here. Some nights, I wake up and swear I see black frost on the windows. Feel it in a room only to turn on the light and it's not there."

Jace met her eyes and brought a hand up to cup her face. "And in the master bedroom that night when you found me with the gun…"

She leaned forward to kiss him. It really had become their way of saying they knew what the other was going to say. No reason to state it any further. With no additional discussion needed. He spoke of the time he almost ended his own life, also a subject neither Kitt nor he wanted to revisit. He'd happily avoid it, kisses or not.

He gave her an appreciative smile, skipped it, and continued. "You were saying how you wanted to have a house that we started our life in together. But you also loved the view. I did too, once. But after Ohio, I may have become slightly anti-water. And now that your parents have moved, do we have a reason not to?"

Kitt chewed on her bottom lip. "But can you? What about the agency? The crew? Not to mention, are you able to with all the legal stuff?" She got to her feet and crossed her arms. "Where are you thinking? I love the water, baby. And I love Texas. I definitely don't want to move to Ohio." They both shook their heads adamantly. Not that state and not any where winter was considered a real season.

Jace rose and pulled her into a hug. "I don't know. Somewhere warm. Some place away from the water, but close enough for you. I know you love it. But there's one other thing."

"What?" Kitt asked with a speculative raised brow.

"The baby's room will still have to be yellow." And that got him a smack.

"Ready to see your baby?"

He and Kitt were in the doctor's office. She would be having their first sonogram. After the scare, their ob-gyn decided to have it now at seven weeks, rather than the normal ten-week point. They had been told it would be far too early for a gender to be seen, but they would be able to see the tiny forming baby within Kitt's womb and hear the heartbeat.

Jace sat next to the hospital bed. He smiled as Kitt giggled from the cold gel put on her still flat stomach. The technician worked the handheld device over Kitt's stomach and Jace's eyes were glued to the monitor.

"There, you see…" The technician pointed to the white and black image. But then, her words halted and she frowned.

Jace had one of his own as the screen went dark except around the edges. It was strange, like an object got in the way of the ultrasound wand and his child.

"Hmm… I thought I had it. But now, I don't know. Hold on." The technician cleaned off the end of the ultrasound and reapplied the gel to Kitt's stomach again.

"Is something wrong?" Kitt asked nervously. Her eyes jerked to Jace's.

He gave her a nervous smile and bent down to kiss her. "It's fine. Bet it's a glitch." His eyes darted back to the monitor. He sat back up as the technician attempted again. He held in a breath. And let it go slowly, when the grey and black live image appeared on the monitor as before.

"There we go." She gave them both a smile. "Technology. It's always keeping us on our toes, right?"

Jace nodded. Kitt let out a small laugh to cover her panic. The trip to the emergency room a fresh memory for them both.

"There's your baby. See?"

Jace stood up to lean across Kitt. She moved a bit sideways to get a closer look too. It wasn't very baby-looking. The woman drew a circle around the small mass. "That? It's so tiny." But Jace's lips curved up in an amazed smile. Kitt giggled with tears as she grabbed for his hand. His had sought hers at the same time and they clasped them together.

The technician gave them both a smile. "It's about the size of a blueberry. Let's see if we can hear the heartbeat." She pressed the ultrasound device a bit deeper on Kitt's stomach and hit a button on the console.

And the most amazing sound filled the room.

The fast-beating sound reminded Jace of a hummingbird in water. "Is it supposed to be that fast?"

The technician nodded as she explained the pace was normal at ninety to one-hundred and ten beats a minute. He laughed and now, he had tears when she told them that everything seemed normal. Kitt pulled him down for a kiss and he returned it, full of emotion. But his eyes were on the monitor. He wanted to keep that thing on Kitt from this moment until they held the baby. It could help him keep both of them safe. He could check on their baby every day and watch him or her grow.

Confirmation of something being normal in Jace's life was a big fucking deal.

"Would you like a printout?"

Both he and Kitt said yes at the same time, full of excitement.

The technician laughed. Jace was sure his and Kitt's behavior was no different than most parents. Parents… holy shit, he was going to be a parent. Some kid's father. The impact of it hit him hard. He had to sit next to the bed with Kitt's hand still in his. His own father had stepped out before Jace had been born. His mother said the man was an asshole. Should be blamed for all the bad that came into Jace's childhood.

With no example to learn from, Jace was going to be a father.

"Baby? Are you okay?"

He wiped his eyes and could only nod in response to Kitt's question. She would have guessed the turmoil of emotions he felt and she leaned over to give him a kiss. No answer needed.

"Here you go. You can get dressed now."

She handed them two print outs of the ultrasound. "Excuse me, uh…" He moved to intercept her exit. "What is this? I don't remember seeing that before."

She took the printed scan and tilted her head. "Oh, that black blur there? Huh. It's nothing, I'm sure. And since I didn't see it on the ultrasound, it's probably something on the printer. I wouldn't worry. We'll print out a new picture at your next appointment." She laughed and patted Jace's arm with a smile. "Most parents want to get one each scan, so they can show it off. And I can tell you two are going to be that type of parents."

Jace had to accept that answer from the professional in the room. His stomach did its strange twisting sensation and for a blink, he felt nauseated. He looked up as Kitt stood to get dressed. The happy smile on her face vanquished the sickening feeling. God, did he love her. He kissed her before he pulled her into a tight hug.

She giggled and returned the hug as she rested her head on his chest. "You know what we should do to celebrate the first pictures of our baby?"

Jace laughed and shook his head. "Let me guess. Shrimp baskets and onion rings?"

She stood on her toes and smiled wide, nose crinkled and all. "Yes. And ice cream on the Strand." She frowned a little. "What if they don't have ice cream in Austin?"

He laughed. "They not only have ice cream, baby. But they have a fudge shop where they sing." And just like that, Jace could tell Austin, Texas just *might* win his beach girl's flip-flopped heart. He had an arm wrapped around her waist as they exited the clinic. Kitt held the photos happily against her chest. They reached his car and he assisted her into the passenger seat, fastening her seat belt. And he stole another kiss before he closed the door. He had reached the driver's side and had his hand on the handle when his name was called out.

"Jace Camden?"

He paused, pivoted to face the building, and found an older man standing there. The man had salt-and-pepper hair and although most likely in his sixties, time had been a friend to him. Jace tilted his head and moved his shades to the top of his head. When Kitt stepped out of the car in curiosity, all his defenses went on alert. She said timidly, as unsure as Jace, "Baby?"

Jace brought his hand up but kept his eyes on the man. "Get back in the car, Kitt."

"Who is that?" Her stubbornness had grown ten-fold since becoming pregnant. She did not get back into the car.

"I have no idea." He darted a sideways glance at her. "But please. Get in the car." She opened her mouth to protest before she lowered herself back inside the vehicle.

Jace hit the door lock button on the BMW fob and took a step towards the man. "Who are you? Do I know you?"

The man had the intelligence and sense to not move from where he stood. "No. You don't. But you should. If I had been allowed my way."

He took a step closer and Jace held up a hand to warn him not to. "No. You stay there." But there was something about the man. Perhaps it was the way he stood or the tense bunching of the man's shoulders even as a calm façade faced outward. Jace's mind felt like it scurried inside of his skull that there was *something* Jace needed to be aware of. A dream that lurked in its grey depths that did not wait for him to sleep to be shone.

So it didn't… A boy in a room. Tied to a bed. And a voice on the other side of the door.

"Just let me take him. Then you don't have to be worried about the demons getting to you. I'll take the boy and you won't have to fight it anymore."

No. It couldn't be. His brain was not always Jace's friend and he actually fucking prayed that this was one of those times. "What's your name?"

"I'm glad the demons didn't get what they wanted. You're alive. I've been looking for you. It wasn't until I saw a write-up in the paper about an incident in Ohio. But you didn't live there. Then I paid a cop to give me your address in Galveston. I followed you from your house. You and the pretty girl. Her name is Kitt Thomas, right?"

Jace snarled and curled his hands into fists. "I said, what the fuck is your name?"

The man gave a gentle and friendly smile. "You don't remember me? It has been a very long time. But I'm not here to hurt you. My name is Jackson." He took another step closer with his arms out to his side, perhaps to present himself as not a threat. Didn't matter, Jace was feeling both threatened and fucking confused so he took a step back. Kitt had moved out of the car and called his name in alarm.

The man took another step. And then another until Jace's back hit the car. He closed his eyes but ears did not have that ability. Jace had little choice in not hearing what came next—even if his mind had already pieced together the puzzle of its meaning.

"Jace, son. I'm your father."

Holy. Shit... Jace thought right before the pavement and blackness came up to meet him.

SNEAK PEEK — SOUL BOUND III: THE WANTED

COMING APRIL 2020
AVAILABLE FOR PREORDER NOW!

PROLOGUE

"Ms. Camden! You have to push. We need you to push! I can see the baby's head. Come on! You can do it!"

Elizabeth, called Liz by her friends, Camden was pushing as the doctor told her. A doctor she did not know as she had not dared to see one before the labor contractions had begun. Driving herself to the hospital, swerving during the pain and righting the car between the spasms, she had pulled up at the closest emergency room and walked inside.

Having filled out the paperwork, they did not ask for any more information which suited Liz just fine. She moved. And she did so often. Powers forced her to. None of the scholarly medical professionals would have had the ability to believe it. They would have thought her insane or dismissed her all together as another homeless woman unhinged. However, Liz was anything but. She was highly intelligent and a survivor. She also knew better than to get pregnant but it only took a few days with a stranger for that to occur. A stranger that made the voices stop. A stranger that for some reason, the demons that began to appear in the last few years seemed scared of. They retreated and hid in the corners but otherwise left her alone with the man who had impregnated her. The value of that was better than the sex—though it was a welcome escape as well.

Liz chose to be homeless for she had to stay on the move—it was better that way for the baby that in that moment seemed very unwilling to leave the haven of her womb.

"Come on, Ms. Camden. One more big push."

One of the nurses moved to help her sit up. Her knees were in the stirrups. Liz's back curled forward as she screamed, her teeth grinding through the pain as her head went downward. Eyes opening as she felt an internal release of pressure. Water with blood splashed on the floor and splattered the doctor standing between her thighs.

The floor was a pale blue and the puddle that shimmered was deep crimson. Liz was transfixed by it. The image reflected in its pool of the baby with a full head of hair emerged from her body—amazing that a human baby could fit from an opening barely able to accommodate the large member of the man that helped Liz create the infant. As the baby's shoulders were followed by its torso another splash of fluid followed.

"It's a boy! Congratulations!" The doctor looked thrilled as she began cutting the umbilical cord. "Did you have a name for your son, Ms. Camden?"

Liz panted, her eyes jerking up as a wave of pain shattered through her. "Jace. His name is Jace. My son's name is Jace…" The pain increased and she curled forward once again to ride it out and her eyes went to the puddle one more. In that moment Liz realized she had housed far more than her son that now squalled with indignation of being stolen from his warm hiding place.

Liz started screaming. The medical staff became alarmed and the nurse at her back moved forward to comfort her. The baby was taken away as the team in the emergency room attempted to calm Liz. It was useless and she threw herself off the bed sending the metal tray of supplies to the floor. She slid and tripped in the bloody mess on the floor and fell against the wall. Dragging the placenta and its shriveling cord behind her. It slid like an engorged worm, squirting blood like it was dying but fought its own end.

Liz pointed as she hysterically tried to form words and snarled when they touched her. Why did they not listen to her! Didn't they realize the evil in the room? Could they not feel it? She could. She always did. A pounding headache and a wave of nausea threatening to overcome her when she was this close to that evil.

It was *right there!* "Don't let it get to the baby! It wants Jace!"

But before the demon made a move to do that—it smiled with long pointed teeth, its skin mottled with both her birth fluids and its own slime—and began eating the dying placenta.

It was the last thing Liz saw before a new alarming set of yells from the staff sounded.

"They are both coding! The baby and the mother! Code Blue! Code Blue!..."

CHAPTER ONE

"Baby, I know why you're doing this. But I can't remember telephone numbers if I've even had them for a year. Much less if we're going to change them every month. Add that to getting lost when I try to drive into Austin, you got to give me a break."

Jace knew Kitt was frustrated. And pregnant. Add those two factors of their life to his obsessive paranoia, she had every right to be. "Yeah, but I got a call that said nothing from a number I don't know twice now. It could be him."

Kitt moved to sit in front of him and he reached up to help her down. She was six months pregnant and if Jace thought she was clumsy before, it was ten-fold as the pregnancy advanced. Now sitting on the ottoman in front of him, she tilted his chin up to meet her eyes. "Jace, you just said could. Which means, it may not be your father. And maybe you should let him at least try to explain."

Jace let out a frustrated growl as he slowly shook his head. "We've discussed this. I do not want Jackson Wallace anywhere near you. Or our baby." Squeezing his eyes shut, he did his usual count to ten to calm down and then slowly blew out an exhale. "Can we not hash through it again. I want to focus on you and our baby. The last thing I need is a man who walked out before I was even born around you two." His eyes opened to meet her hazel gaze full of concern. "Around me.

I've lived to be in my thirties and it's a bit too late for him to want to play daddy, okay?"

Rising to his feet, Jace raked his fingers through his hair and hoped that it would be that easy for his girlfriend to drop a subject he had made very clear he did not wish to discuss. Hope was a bitch and never on Jace's side—this time would not be any different.

Kitt wobbled to her feet with one hand on her baby belly as she moved to block his retreat from the room. "I know. But I also know he did a lot of work to try to find you. If he didn't want to be in your life, after all these years, why would he do that? Don't you at least want to know that?"

Jace opened his mouth to protest but a knock rapped on the screen door of their simple San Marcos house. They had been lucky to find it—thanks to a friend of Zane's grandfather. The house was simple but it rested on the bank of the Guadalupe River and just ten miles outside of town South. They had San Antonio less than a half-hour away and Austin just thirty miles to their North. And not only had he and Kitt relocated to Central Texas but the whole Dead Man's Crew had come along as well.

Looking over at the door, he let out a soft curse as they had been interrupted by those same people now. "Do you all have no concept of calling before you show up? A text? Shit, I don't know even considering we might be busy?"

Skylar, flippant as always, threw open the door and gave him a smile. "We are well aware of common courtesy and how to be polite. We just don't do that for you." She walked inside and gave Kitt a hug before putting her arm around Jace's girlfriend's waist. "Hey beautiful. Is he being an asshole again?" She smirked and gave him a glare. "It's not healthy to be a dick to a pregnant woman, Jace. Speaking of manners."

Zane, Alex and Franklin filed in and Jace met Kitt's gaze. Perhaps he should be glad they had decided to show up—it was a much-needed delay on the heated argument about to break out between him and Kitt on the subject of his father.

"What makes you think I'm being a dick, Sky?" Jace crossed his arms on his chest and narrowed his gaze. "I can be nice. Even loving."

"Isn't loving what got her pregnant? Or was it some angry sex? Angry sex is good. Maybe that's why I like being with you." Zane tilted his head to give Skylar a smile. "You hate me. But the sex is great." He started laughing as he stood behind Skylar. A woman he just called his girlfriend. Even more baffling to Jace was that Skylar let him do it. Bizarre. Jace knew that word well and never thought it lightly. But Zane and Skylar being a couple still merited the description.

Jace groaned and dropped his chin to his chest. "Can we add your two's sex life to the ever-growing list of subject matter we will not nor want to discuss?" He lifted just his eyes and sighed. "Just thought I'd ask. You guys have zero respect for that list now. What makes me think that would change?"

THE WANTED IS COMING APRIL 2020

Make sure you are one of the first to

#SB3SurviveWanted

with the twisting, exciting finale of the Soul Bound Trilogy

Soul Bound III: The Wanted

You Can Order It Here:

https://books2read.com/SoulBound3

Join Ward's Newsletter here for exclusive FIRST LOOKS & Other

Member Exclusive Content:

www.AuthorJasTWard.com

If you enjoyed this book, we invite you to download a FREE taste of her exciting Shadow-Keeper Series with BOUNCE: A Story from the Grid. Find out how on Ward's website!

www.AuthorJasTWard.com

As a special gift – read a sneak peek of ENVY NOW!

Turn the page and get infected on The Grid today.

ENVY

Book Five: The Shadow-Keepers Series

By Jas T. Ward

Prologue

The old woman's voice had droned on for more than an hour but Epsilon needed not the words but her money; he hid his irritation well. Six months had gone by since his father, the dark ruler of hell, Lucifer had cut off any assistance—which included funds to supplement Epsilon's army. In that time, he had used his trained mercenaries and soldiers to take on certain unsavory tasks.

"I was told you were discreet."

The woman wound down her personal history and Epsilon smiled as he ran his fingers down the pressed crease of his trousers. Slowly flexing his hand before he clasped it in the other in his lap, he gave her a slow smile. "I am. And I am sure you would expect that to continue with this task. However, Mrs. Shen, you must also presume that my services do not come cheap. You were told that as well?"

The Asian woman's steely stare must have intimidated everyone she had ever placed in its sights but not Epsilon—one was not the son of Lucifer and shriveled in front of any human. Much less an elderly one almost seventy-years-old.

Mrs. Shen stood, the expensive linen of her gray suit swishing with the smoothness of her moves. "Mr. White, my marriage was one of arrangement between two of the wealthiest families in our region. I accepted that and did not complain. I assisted my husband when our families' companies combined, and he took charge of the operations."

She angled to look back at him, her gaze scathing like he stood there with shit on his shoe, marring up the expensive rug on the floor under it.

"Without me, Shen Enterprises would not exist. Our fathers died and my husband inherited everything. And I accepted that as well. When I gave birth to my son, the only male to carry on the family business, that too, I accepted. It was the way of our culture. However, when my son and his wife died in the plane crash." Her eyes moved away from Epsilon and he tilted his head to attempt to detect some grief in her tone. But no, even though the plan crash occurred less than a year ago, she sounded just as cold about the death of her son as the rest of her history.

Completely without emotion.

A living, aging statue.

"I should have been given control. Finally, given control of what I built. Built not by grooming the men in my life, but by manipulating and controlling them. By whispering in their ears, the best decisions and knowing they would follow as if they had hatched the plans. But no…" Epsilon had been incorrect about the lack of emotion, hate and vengeful venom tainted her words now. "My son gave control of the entire Shen empire to a seventeen-year-old child." Her palm slammed down on the table in front of her. The impact so hard the lovely tiny carvings chinked together like individual wind chimes made of china.

"Ah," Epsilon stood to approach her and smiled. "A trust fund that converts when your granddaughter, Jade, turns eighteen." He tilted his head. "I did my research. Your son and his wife died in a private crash over the mountains of Montana. And he left your funds, the companies, the properties, everything except your living allowance and this home, to his daughter. That must have hurt. To finally have a chance to hold the reins of a very powerful steed and they are given to a little girl."

"She is a child! A shy, withdrawn, witless child. She has no confidence and loses herself inside of books! Not even intelligent reads but ridiculous volumes of fantasy and fiction. Her father let her go to public school with children of low class! Not a school that would groom her for the role to be a woman of power! Nor a wife worthy of a powerful man! Just a girl. He allowed her to just be..." she spat out the word like it tasted like the imagined shit on his shoe, "just herself. No pressure. No training and she is not *suitable* nor worthy of what I built, Mr. White!" She brought her palm up to her chest, which was rising and falling with deep indignation like she had ran to get herself worked up. "And he leaves it all to *her!*"

Epsilon reached out to take her hand and stroked his thumb over her wrinkled knuckles, lifting his eyes to hers. "And if she dies, you finally have it all."

Her eyes met his and Epsilon found her gaze like that of a viper who had been contained in its basket for too long and wanted to sink its fangs into its charmer's throat. "Yes. I was told you would do this. That the factor of being a child would be no issue. And if you researched, you know I can pay whatever fee you wish. As long as you do this deed."

Epsilon brought her hand up to kiss her knuckles with a deadly smile, meeting her eyes. "I can. And the fee will be one of your son's companies."

"Which one?" Her face went emotionless once more, and the coldness had returned to her tone.

Epsilon pulled out a piece of paper and pressed it into her hand as he released it. "The one in Columbia that makes weapons."

"Ms. Shen, we're here."

Jade pulled her earbuds out when the driver announced they had arrived at her grandmother's home. She hated the rambling mansion above the city with its empty rooms, servants and ghosts of the past. She hated her room which was not allowed to be changed from its museum type interior—as the rest of the house. The only rooms Jade found any solace in were her grandfather's library and the solarium it opened into. She never knew the man as he had died when her father was a teenager. Sighing as she tucked away her well-worn copy of The Hunger Games paperback in her messenger bag, followed by her phone and earbuds, she mumbled a thank you and exited the sedan. Watching the private driver round the corner to park the car, she let her head fall forward, her eyes sliding over in puzzlement at the car parked on the curb with a large, intimidating man standing next to it.

Someone was visiting her grandmother? Strange, the woman ran over the schedule every morning over breakfast and had said nothing about any appointments.

Walking up the steps to the front door, she entered and dropped her bag by the front door. "Soba? I'm home. Do we have company?"

"Hello, Jade."

A person moved in front of her and she creased her brow in confusion as her eyes trailed up expensive suit jacket buttons, over a deep blue tie and then continued upward to meet startling blue eyes. They were the hue of an iceberg—harmless on the surface but the danger far below, underneath. "Hello?"

The man smiled and something about it had Jade stepping back only to hit the large man from outside as he entered the home. "Soba?" Her breath hitched and fear made the hair on the back of her neck stand like someone, or something was whispering in silence against her skin. A warning she could not hear.

The man in the suit stepped close to her and Jade tried to avoid his hand as it came up to touch her chin and fingers clasped it brutally.

"You are a pretty one. What a shame such a pretty doll is about to die."

Grab the whole series and catch up today!

Preorder Envy to get infected in January of 2020:

https://books2read.com/WardsEnvy

ACKNOWLEDGEMENTS

This trilogy is the hardest I ever would have thought to write. But yet, you readers have welcomed my dark, twisted love story. And thank you for that.

<u>To my family:</u> To those that have supported me and my books—thank you. For those that did not, it's too late now. Go read something happy and fluffy.

<u>To Team Ward:</u> How you put up with me and try to keep me on track and schedule, I honestly don't know. But you deserve combat pay for doing so. Here's hoping we sell lots of books so I can do that. Until then, thank you so much. You help take the pressure off so I can write. Imagine so many hearty things here.

<u>To RJ Loom:</u> The worst best friend ever. Meanness does not equal love. But you know what, I'll take it anyway.

<u>To my amazing artsy people, Lori, Lisa Jane, Rachel and Amy including the amazing Carolann (and our Little Keeper):</u> What would I do without you? You make my books look so wonderful with covers and teasers. And I have no idea how you pluck the images in my overly active, cluttered brain and make such works of book themed art. Thank you for making The Ward Way look so damn good.

<u>To my readers group, The Grid Nights & the Inner Squad and the Crazy Ladies:</u> Wow. You ladies and gentlemen amaze me with your

encouragement, support and just wanting to read what's written. It floors me and humbles me to think you give one single grain of damn for what I do. I would have never published one single book without you guys. Thank you, thank you, and thank you.

Find the groups here:
https://www.facebook.com/groups/OriginalNightsFanGroup/ &
https://www.facebook.com/groups/TheCrazyReaders/

<u>Girls Gone Writing, Fellow Authors & Bloggers:</u> I am so honored to be in such an amazing, cross-promoting and supporting community of talent. Not to mention, pretty cool people too. Thank you for at least trying to understand how I work. Or, some days, don't work. I know I'm not the easiest to get and somedays I am confusing as ______. But as fellow authors and peers, you didn't find it too much of a challenge and I've found some kindred spirits, family and friends.

Join us here:
https://www.facebook.com/groups/GirlsGoneWriting/

<u>Finally – this one goes to myself:</u> You're a Rockstar… tell yourself that every damn day. Even when the inner voice tells you it's bullshit. Tell it to shut up and shine.

About the Author

"Why the Ward Way? Because I believe in writing books that take a reader on a thrill-ride. Action, danger, drama, sure. But also laughter, tears of joy and moments that make you want to stop just to scream. My books are twisted, complex and full of heroes and heroines full of flaws and heart, but a reader cannot deny--total badasses. Welcome to my worlds, take a seat, get to know me and the characters and I assure you... You'll be glad you did." ~Jas T Ward

Born and raised in Texas, Ward is a mixed bag of creativity spinning tales of paranormal, urban fantasy and even dark romance and horror; wrapped within a love story. She's been dared to write a few contemporary romances but even those reads have characters that are real and twisted by their creator.
Mother of three diverse and independent bold children, Ward prides herself for being the "Queen Niche' Bitch" which is a handy way of saying she sucks writing to market.
But her readers don't seem to mind.

Ms. Ward is can be reached via social media at:

Website: http://www.authorjastward.com/
Facebook: https://www.facebook.com/AuthorJasTWard

SOCIAL MEDIA LINKS
Goodreads: http://bit.ly/JASTWARDGR
Twitter: https://twitter.com/JasTWard
BookBub: https://www.bookbub.com/authors/jas-t-ward

215

FROZEN CHILDREN

A Memoir of
Remembering, Forgiving, Letting Go, and Living

SHELLEY JOHNSON

Frozen Children
Copyright © 2019 by Shelley Johnson.

All rights reserved. Printed in the United States of America. No part of this book may be used or reproduced in any manner whatsoever without written permission except in the case of brief quotations embodied in critical articles or reviews.

From the author:
"This book is based on my childhood memories, resurfaced memories, journals and notes, as well as conversations with friends and family. Some names have been changed for privacy reasons. Memory is not infallible, and some descriptions may be flawed, but have been written as I remember them. All I have are memories and no 'proof' that many of the events took place. I recognize and acknowledge that some members of my family do not have the same memories or beliefs about my childhood as I do. I believe everything written to be true and have published this book in the hope of aiding my own healing as well as that of others that may read it. This is a book of healing and of hope. It is not intended to bring hurt or embarrassment to anyone."

For information contact:
http://www.frozenchildren.com

Edited by Nanette Littlestone

First Edition - August 2019

ISBN: 978-0-9983661-1-1